THE MYSTERY OF WATERMEAD MANOR

HENRY FLEMING INVESTIGATES
BOOK TWO

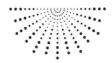

JAY GILL

VISIT WWW.JAYGILL.NET

Visit my website for new releases and special offers: www.jaygill.net

WELCOME NOTE

Welcome readers, old and new. I'm excited to share with you the second *Henry Fleming Investigates* mystery. Though part of a series, each book can be read as a standalone. This mystery, as with the others in the series, is spoiler-free so you won't find out the killer from any previous investigation and, in the very best tradition of the whodunnit story, the cast of characters, along with a smattering of red-herrings, will have you guessing until the end, when our great detective presides over his *grand reveal*.

Though the story is set in England 1923, for the purpose of readability, I have taken certain liberties with the language, customs and behaviour of the day, some of which we now consider outdated. My aim is entertainment, rather than strict adherence to historical fact.

The *Henry Fleming Investigates* series is a clean read with no graphic violence, bedroom shenanigans, or strong language.

Towards the back of the book, you will find details of the next mystery in the series, plus mention of a free Henry Fleming short story.

And so, without further ado, let's examine *The Mystery of Watermead Manor*.

Cast List

Henry Fleming (Private detective)

Skip (Fleming's four-legged friend. Yellow Labrador)

Mrs Clayton (Fleming's housekeeper)

Inspector Carp

Lord Anthony Dalton

Gerald and Ida Langley

Lady Mary Stafford

Joyce Toule

Mrs Margaret Winters (Joyce's governess)

Vincent Ackerman (Gerald's accountant)

Sir Peter Upton (Explorer)

Dr Robert Singer

Major Digby Fielding (Retired)

Stanley Barnes (Butler)

Tilly Caster (Maid)

Alfred Mason (Footman)

Mr Taylor (Chauffeur)

An Extract from the Diary of
H. K. Fleming, Esq.

Watermead Manor, 1923

I have arrived at Watermead Manor as a guest of my good friend Lord Anthony Dalton. The estate does not disappoint and on first impressions, despite Anne's passing and the loss of her personal touch, the house and gardens remain immaculate. Her legacy lives on!

From the little I have seen so far, the extensive grounds too are in fine condition and I'm looking forward to some time walking and reacquainting myself with the estate's treasures. The rose garden, of course, is of particular interest, and I hope to track down the head gardener to exchange notes.

The weather is agreeable for the time of year.

My recent correspondence and subsequent meeting with Anthony at the country club, made it obvious to me that my friend puts on a brave face, and my dearest hope is that our time together brings him some cheer. Without his beloved Anne he remains a broken man. I fear he is lonely, and rudderless – a condition with which I too am

well acquainted and have expressed privately within these very pages.

His other guests have certainly provided a welcome distraction. My own spirits have been lifted to see the guests of honour, Gerald and his new wife, Ida. They make a handsome couple. Gerald has grown into a striking young gentleman, and I am filled with pride on his parents' behalf. I hope to converse more with them both in due course.

There has been a murder! Wickedness incarnate stalks Watermead Manor and my words fail me. I must think! Think! I have little time but many questions. There is much work to be done. If ever I must be up to the task, it is now!

CHAPTER ONE

ENGLAND, 1923

Lord Anthony Dalton had been reclining in his favourite armchair at the country club, reading that morning's edition of *The Times*. He'd read only a couple of pages when Fleming arrived. He quickly folded the paper, placed it on the coffee table beside him and stood to greet his friend.

'Henry, my dear chap. How good to see you. Thank you for coming at such short notice.'

He smoothed his thinning blond hair and smiled broadly, hoping his blue eyes didn't betray how empty he felt inside. He was genuinely delighted to see Fleming and mustered as much enthusiasm as he could manage.

'Good to see you too, Anthony. You're looking well.'

Henry Fleming was a handsome man, of average height and build, with warm brown eyes that Lord Dalton believed missed nothing. His hair was greying and slightly receding at the temples. He was, as usual, immaculately dressed in a perfectly fitting three-piece suit, no doubt from his favourite Savile Row tailors, Buford & Doyle.

Fleming had been about to return to London from Avonbrook Cottage, in Shinton Moor, when he received an urgent telegram. Despite being pressed for time, and the country club being a little out of his way, his old friend's request for a drink and private conversation had intrigued him, so he had decided to make the detour.

Outside, an afternoon downpour brought with it a cold chill but, at Lord Dalton's behest, the club had prepared the fireplace which now cracked and popped invitingly as the heat intensified and the flames grew.

Lord Dalton opened his cigarette case and offered it to Fleming, which he declined.

'I should stop,' he said, snapping the case closed. He put a cigarette to his lips, lit it and winked. 'After this one, perhaps.'

Anthony Dalton returned to his armchair and waved Henry to the one next to him.

Fleming watched his friend closely. 'What's on your mind, Anthony?'

Lord Dalton chuckled. 'So few people call me by my first name these days, it feels odd to hear it now. Anne used to, of course.' He stared at the warming fire as he recalled the sound of her voice.

'She called you many things, as I remember,' Fleming replied with a smile. 'Some of which shouldn't be repeated in polite company.'

'She hated my smoking.' Lord Dalton held the cigarette aloft. 'She certainly knew how to keep me in my place.' He laughed.

'Men without purpose or direction will behave like boys if left to their own devices. For a while, you had little purpose, and certainly no direction.'

'She kept me in line, that's for sure.'

'A fine woman will, my friend. And Anne was certainly that.'

Lord Dalton regarded Fleming fondly. 'Yes, she was the finest.' He smoked his cigarette in silence for a moment. 'What do you make of Gerald Langley's marriage to Ida, Henry?'

'What I know of Gerald, and from what you've told me of Ida, they'll make a grand couple.' Fleming watched as his lordship tossed his cigarette end into the fire and lit another.

Lord Dalton nodded in agreement. 'I suppose they will. I hope Gerald treats her well.'

'Why shouldn't he?'

'I don't know the lad as well as yourself, of course, but I'm aware of the tragic loss of his parents when he was just a boy. His rebellious teenage years. The inheritance of his parents' fortune at twenty-one. The drinking. I'm informed he's something of a ladies' man. While Ida, on the other hand, is...' He groped around for the correct words. 'She's quite something.'

'Were you any different in your youth, Anthony?' Fleming asked. 'How many times in your early years were you drunk and in love? Often, I might add, with a woman whose company had been paid for?'

Lord Dalton released a large puff of smoke and laughed heartily. 'You make me sound very caddish.'

'You were a rich, rebellious, hard drinking ladies' man. Until you met Anne.'

'Yes, I suppose I was. Until I met Anne...

'I just hope Gerald realises what he has with Ida and changes his ways. She deserves someone who'll look after her and treat her well. When you meet her, you'll know what I mean.'

'Would you like me to look in on them both from time to time?'

Lord Dalton grinned. 'That's a great idea.'

'You could have just asked.'

'I like to think I'm rather more devious than you. Able to subtly *suggest* so you become convinced it was your idea.'

Fleming shook his head and laughed. 'In truth, your art of suggestion, which I saw straight through, felt a little like a toddler playing chess. Clumsy.'

'Am I really that transparent?'

'Only to me, my friend. I know you too well,' Fleming said. Then with a straight face and a wink, he added, 'I'm also Britain's greatest detective.'

The two laughed even louder at the shared joke. *The Times* on the coffee table was open on an exaggerated account of Fleming's art of detection. It covered a recent case and posed the question: Should Henry Fleming be heralded as 'Britain's greatest detective'?

'I've invited Ida and Gerald, together with a few other guests, to spend next weekend at Watermead Manor, I've planned a few celebratory dinners, hired a jazz band and what have you. It's short notice I know, but I'd like you to be there.'

Fleming sighed and spoke in a whisper. 'This case in London is a matter of national importance. I'd welcome a weekend at the estate and, should I be finished, I'd love to join you, but I can't make any promises.'

'I understand. This business in Europe has everyone on edge. The repercussions of the war can still be felt. Do what you can. You're always welcome at Watermead.'

CHAPTER TWO

'I still can't believe it,' Joyce Toule said. 'Married?' She looked up at her friend who stood several inches taller. Ida flicked back her long dark hair. She was tall, slim, and elegant; everything Joyce wanted to be.

Lord Dalton had offered Ida and Gerald Watermead Manor's finest room. From the window there were panoramic views across the lawns and gardens to the boating lake in the distance.

Ida giggled and pulled her friend close. Standing back, she held up her hand once again to show off the wedding ring on her finely-shaped finger. 'I can't believe it either, but it's true. I'm officially Mrs Gerald Langley.'

'Mrs Gerald Langley. It has a wonderful ring to it,' sighed Joyce.

'Yes, can you believe it? He doesn't care a jot about my not coming from money. He said he has enough for the both of us, and plenty more besides. I adore him more than words can say.'

'I'm annoyed with you, of course.' Joyce frowned playfully. 'I wasn't invited to the wedding.'

'Nobody was. It was just Gerald and me and a few strangers he paid to witness it all. It felt deliciously daring. His godmother, Lady Stafford, is outraged, of course.'

'That old battle-axe looks terrifying.'

'She's monstrous. She's made our lives a misery every day since we returned. There's a constant atmosphere at Chippingwood Hall. Gerald's even talking about asking her to leave.'

'That would be awful. He wouldn't do that, surely?' said Joyce.

'It's what she deserves. She's been extremely rude to me on a number of occasions and Gerald won't stand for it. But we mustn't let her spoil this weekend together. We'll ignore her, that's what we'll do.' Ida jumped for joy and spun around. 'I'm bursting with excitement.'

'I'm so happy for you. I knew he liked you from the moment we met him at the Southern Summer Ball, but I never imagined it would end in a whirlwind romance on another continent. I need to hear every detail.'

'I'll tell you all later. Right now, though, we're late.' Ida slipped into her dress and turned around. Joyce fastened the back for her.

'What about you? Any romance on the cards?'

'Nothing to write home about,' Joyce pouted. She pointed to one of the haute couture dresses laid out on the bed. 'Certainly nobody rich and handsome like Gerald. Just how rich is he, anyway?'

Ida slipped on her new heels and then, having brought her hair over her shoulders, stood back and looked in the mirror. 'Obscenely so, and he loves nothing more than showering me with gifts.' She opened a jewellery box and took out a string of pearls.

Joyce's eyes widened. 'Oh my goodness! Are they real?'

'Every one of them. Look, matching earrings.' Ida took out two large pearls and sat on the edge of the bed while Joyce knelt behind her to help with the clasp of the necklace.

'I knew you'd land on your feet,' Joyce said. 'You're so beautiful and clever. Men have always fallen over themselves to have you on their arm.'

Ida turned and faced her friend. 'You'll find some-one, I promise. I'll introduce you to all of Gerald's friends. We'll have you married in no time.'

Joyce sighed. 'I also want to travel like you. Africa – it sounds so romantic.'

'In that case, we'll find a man who's full of adventure, just like my Gerald.'

Joyce smiled again. 'Yes. And we'll marry at sunset in front of Mount Kilimanjaro. With zebras carrying canapes and champagne. The guests will arrive on enormous elephants with huge tusks.'

Ida laughed and shook her head. 'Your imagination's still as vivid as ever. You're still that funny dear friend I've known my whole life.' She squeezed Joyce again. 'This won't change our friendship, you know.'

'I hope not, though I've a feeling it might. Now you've moved to Chippingwood Hall and you're surrounded by servants, with acres of land between you and rest of the world, you won't have time for girlish silliness and dreaming. That life belonged to Ida Newbury, not the wealthy Mrs Gerald Langley.'

Ida took Joyce's hand. 'I promise you, with my life,' she said seriously, 'that I'll always have time for you. Nothing will ever change the fact that you're my best friend and like the sister I never had. We'll always look out for each other and I'll be there for you, no matter what, I swear it.' She smiled lovingly at Joyce, lifted her chin and kissed her on the forehead. 'Now, choose a dress. Any dress. I want you to wear whatever you want.'

'Oh! I couldn't possibly. They must have cost a fortune. What will Gerald say?'

Ida jumped to her feet. 'He won't know. He can't remember from one day to the next what he's bought me.' She went back to her jewellery box and took out a diamond necklace, which she passed to Joyce. 'Put this on as well.'

Joyce ran around the bed to the mirror and held it to her neck. 'It's too much! What if I lose it?' She gasped at the way it sparkled. 'It's so beautiful.'

'It's yours. I want you to have it. Call it a wedding gift. Compensation for not being my bridesmaid the way we'd wanted.'

Joyce took it off and handed it back. 'No, Ida. I can't take it.'

'You can't refuse something given as a gift! Anyway, you never know when you might bump into your future husband and need to impress.'

'There's nobody here this weekend that's eligible. Lord Dalton's only invited stuffy old people.'

'Stop making excuses. I want to see you in the dress and wearing your new necklace.'

The clock on the mantelpiece chimed.

'Seven o'clock!' Ida gasped. 'Hurry up, Joyce. We're in so much trouble. Lord Dalton's a stickler for time keeping.'

THE RED OPEN-TOP sports car zig-zagged along the narrow country road. Vincent Ackerman, plump and sweating profusely, closed his eyes and gripped the seat for dear life as they launched over a small stone bridge.

Raising his voice over the sound of the engine, Gerald shouted, 'Incredible, isn't she?' The handsome millionaire laughed as he pushed the accelerator to the floor.

Ackerman dare not open his eyes. 'Very impressive. Corners well. How much further?' he quavered.

'We're nearly there, old chap.'

'Perhaps we can slow down a bit now?' He feared his shredded nerves might never recover.

'I can't slow down. We're late,' Gerald yelled. 'I meant Ida's incredible. Not the car. Though that's phenomenal too.'

Ackerman yelped as Gerald threw the roadster into a hard left turn. They skidded through the entrance of Watermead Manor, the back end sliding and narrowly missing a huge stone gate post. They slowed a little, but not much, and Ackerman dared to open one eye.

'You spend too long with numbers, my friend,' Gerald said. 'You need to live a little.'

'I'm an accountant. I feel comfortable with

numbers. They're safe; reliable. You should try it sometime.'

Gerald laughed at his friend's pale complexion. 'I've no interest in numbers. That's why I pay you.'

As they reached the gravel outside the imposing front doors, Gerald grabbed the handbrake and squealed to a halt. 'There! We made it. That was fun, wasn't it?' He slapped Ackerman on the back and, without opening the door, jumped out onto the drive. 'Are you coming, Ackers?'

Ackerman held up a hand. 'I'll be along in a moment. I need the contents of my stomach to settle first.'

Gerald laughed and bounded up the steps to the main entrance, where Stanley Barnes, the butler, was waiting. Gerald tossed him the car keys.

'Thank you, sir,' Barnes said. 'Mrs Langley's preparing for dinner. She's in her room with Miss Joyce Toule. Some of the guests have arrived and are gathered in the drawing room. Would you like me to take your coat, sir?'

'No, thank you, Barnes, my man. I'll head upstairs and check on my wife.'

'Very good, sir. I'll inform Lord Dalton of your return. Will there be anything else?'

'Perhaps you'd be so kind as to prepare an Old Fashioned for me, and champagne for the ladies.' As he strode away, he said over his shoulder, 'I'll be changed, and ready for dinner, in a flash.'

'Of course, sir.' Barnes placed the car keys in his pocket.

Vincent Ackerman's colour had returned but with legs like jelly he rested a hand on Barnes' shoulder to keep himself steady. 'Which way's the bar?' he enquired shakily.

'This way, sir. I won't take you to the drawing room. You appear a little out of sorts.'

'More than a little, I can tell you.'

'I sense your journey wasn't an entirely pleasant one?'

Ackerman shook his head. 'It was awful. I swear the man has a death wish.'

'The new motorcar does appear rather... brisk?'

'That's an understatement.' Ackerman followed Barnes to the study.

'It's certainly not ideal for the faint of heart,' said Barnes. 'I feel sure I wouldn't enjoy racing along the narrow roads around here either, sir. As a younger man, I took a trip to Italy on a motorcycle. This was before I met Mrs Barnes, of course. It was in my army days. I discovered the roads, especially in the mountains, were little more than dirt tracks. If you're unfortunate enough to make a miscalculation, it's entirely possible to plummet over the edge to certain death.'

Ackerman put up a shaky hand for Barnes to desist.

'Apologies, sir. I wasn't thinking.' Barnes tried to hide his smile. He poured a large single malt and handed it to Ackerman, who'd slumped in a leather armchair. 'There we go, sir. Will there be anything else?'

Ackerman shook his head. 'I'll drink this then change for dinner.'

'I'll inform Lord Dalton.'

CHAPTER THREE

The drawing room was filled with the noise of conversation, giving Lady Mary Stafford one of her dizzy spells.

'Dr Singer, I hope you'll forgive me, but I really must sit down for a moment.' The heavily made-up, and bejewelled baroness, leaned heavily on her walking stick.

'Of course, Lady Stafford. It's quite warm in here. Please, allow me to help you.' Robert Singer put down his drink, smiled warmly and offered his arm.

The baroness took it and together they found a seat in the corner. 'Thank you, Doctor. You know, you look like you haven't eaten in days. You need a good meal inside you.'

'I'm not a big eater,' said the doctor.

'I can see that. You're practically skin and bone.

You really should make more of an effort. Now, don't let me keep you. A young man such as yourself, doesn't want to be stuck chatting to an old lady all evening. You've been far too obliging already. Listening to my ramblings about my thankless godson and his impetuous nature. As I mentioned, the fact Gerald married that girl on a whim, is a prime example of why there should be a law against young men making such decisions without first consulting their elders.'

Dr Singer smiled politely. 'She's a very attractive young woman.'

'Of course she is! That illustrates my point perfectly. I don't wish to appear coarse but young men of Gerald's age are hot-blooded, and I know all too well what's on their mind most of the time.' She pursed her lips disapprovingly. 'You're a man of medicine. You know exactly what I'm talking about.'

'I think I take your meaning,' he murmured, his face reddening.

'You're different, of course. Your family, I'm sure, must be proud of your accomplishments. You've dedicated yourself to your profession.'

'I certainly studied hard, Lady Stafford.' Dr Singer glanced over his shoulder, hoping he might be rescued.

'I should have insisted he take up a profession,' her ladyship continued with a scowl, thumping the floor with her walking stick. 'Medicine, the law, or the military. Had he done something worthwhile with his time, we wouldn't be in the mess in which we find ourselves today – married to a penniless scheming hussy. As far as I can tell, she had no proper chaperone. Unspeakable! It would never have happened in my day I can tell you, and it's all my fault. I gave him the benefit of the doubt and allowed him to travel. How was I so foolish? I can only blame myself. He's always been wilful. As a young boy, he never listened. His father was the same, you know. God rest his soul. Did I tell you about the time...'

'I'm sorry to interrupt,' said Margaret Winters. 'I wonder if I might borrow the doctor for a moment?'

Lady Stafford looked down her nose at Mrs Winters. 'I was just explaining to the good doctor how it fills my heart with joy to see my godson finally married. Such a fine woman and close friend of your Joyce.' Her smile was pained. 'Isn't that right, Doctor?'

The doctor seized his opportunity to escape. 'Absolutely. Please excuse me, Lady Stafford.'

'Come this way, Doctor. I have a question for you.' Once they were out of earshot, Mrs Winters turned to Dr Singer and whispered in his ear. 'She's a liar. That powdered old windbag hates Ida, doesn't she?'

'Well, um.' The doctor felt he may have jumped out of the frying pan straight into the fire.

Mrs Winters laughed, passed him a whisky sour

from the sideboard and took one for herself. 'Don't worry, I'm pulling your leg.' She winked at him. 'From what I've seen, the woman's a snob. She looked down her nose at Joyce and me from the moment we met her. I'm quite sure nobody's ever been good enough for that old crow. I'm as happy as a pig in mud that Ida ruffles the old trout's feathers. If Ida and Gerald are happy, then that's good enough for me.' She clinked her glass with his. 'I'll celebrate that all day long.'

She looked the doctor up and down. 'Drink up, Doctor, I plan on having a few of these and I dislike drinking alone.'

Dr Singer did as he was told. He drained the glass and shuddered as it hit the back of his throat.

'Good lad,' said Mrs Winters. 'Here's another.'

'I don't know if I should.'

'Poppycock! I aim to loosen you up. Too much study makes Robert a dull boy.' She slapped his back and caught the maid's attention. 'Tilly, would you be a sweetheart and get some more of these? Tell whoever's making them to be generous with the whisky.' She raised a roguish eyebrow at Tilly and took the last two glasses. 'I've been told I can let my hair down this weekend and I plan on doing just that. Who says only the youngsters should have all the fun?!'

'Yes, Mrs Winters.' Tilly filled the tray with empty glasses and left the room.

'Cheer up, Robert,' Mrs Winters demanded. 'I heard from Joyce that you and Ida had a thing for a while. As I understand it, you had more of thing for her, than she did for you. Take my advice and forget it. She was never going to end up a doctor's wife. Your paths were destined to go their own ways. Since the day she met my Joyce, I knew she wouldn't stop until she got what she wanted. It seems she finally managed it.'

'I'm pleased for her and Gerald. Really, I am. He's a fine man, I'm sure. He's wealthy, handsome, adventurous. In truth, he's everything I'm not.' He took a large gulp of his second whisky sour. 'I'm okay with that.'

'You're being hard on yourself. I think you had a lucky escape. A woman like Ida would have eaten a chap like you alive. You need to find yourself a more suitable young woman. You're quite the catch. If I were thirty years younger, I'd be making eyes at you myself.'

Robert, who had just taken a mouthful of whisky, coughed and spluttered at the suggestion.

Mrs Winters laughed, loudly. 'I'll have you know, I was quite the looker in my younger days.'

The doctor examined his glass carefully. 'I think there was something in my drink. A piece of lemon, perhaps.'

'Seriously, Robert. Relax. Take a leaf out of my

book and have a good time. Treat each day like it's a party and you'll be as good as gold.'

Mrs Winters left Robert alone as she went in search of the maid and her next whisky sour.

Major Digby Fielding and Sir Peter Upton immediately called the doctor to join them.

'The situation is this,' said Major Fielding, rubbing his large nose and raising his enormous, bushy eyebrows. 'Sir Peter believes that education and financial aid is what's needed in many of these overseas countries that we British govern.'

Sir Peter pushed back his broad shoulders. With his tanned face and unruly hair, he looked like the outdoors-type and appeared uncomfortable with the restrictions of a formal jacket and tie. 'These countries could and should govern themselves,' insisted Sir Peter. 'I've been around the world on many an expedition and seen what a little help can achieve.'

Major Fielding shook his head. 'While I, on the other hand, am a firm believer that while education and financial aid are all well and good, many of these countries would, without a doubt, dissolve into anarchy should we remove our governance.' He jabbed a finger at Robert to emphasise the point. 'It's boots on the ground that ensure law and order. It enables trade between nations, and a semblance of civilised society. Where do you sit in this debate, Doctor?'

The two men stared at him for an answer. Sir Peter's big blue eyes searched the doctor's for reason, while the major anticipated only agreement.

The doctor was about to make an excuse and say something along the lines of needing to give the subject some thought when Ida and Gerald appeared at the drawing room doors. The doctor realised he'd gasped when his eyes fell on Ida. He looked around to make sure nobody had heard.

Ida glided into the room where all eyes fell on her. Her hair was up to reveal her elegant neck and fine shoulders. The dress flowed as she moved to greet guests and the doctor's attention was caught by the huge diamond engagement ring, and the wedding band, on her slender finger. Had he needed to see it to believe it, the truth of her marriage to Gerald was there in front of him. He turned away as they approached.

'Robert,' Ida called. She swooped in and kissed his cheek. 'You made it. Gerald, meet Robert. Robert, this is my husband Gerald.'

'Pleasure to meet you, Robert, old chap.' Gerald gripped his hand and shook it enthusiastically.

'Robert's a childhood friend. He's the sweetest man you'll ever meet. He's also a successful Harley Street doctor.'

Gerald smiled broadly. 'Harley Street's where the money is. You're a smart fellow. You must have brains and money in abundance. I'll be sure to look you up next time I'm in London.'

'I'm certainly a doctor. I suppose I must have some brains, but I certainly don't have much money,' he said awkwardly.

'I don't believe a word of it,' Gerald joked. 'I know how much you London doctors charge.'

'I may not be on Harley Street much longer.'

'Really?' Ida said.

'Why would you jump off that gravy train?' asked Gerald.

'Medicine isn't all about the money.'

'Of course it is. In the end, everything comes down to money.'

'Money can't buy happiness.'

'That's where you're wrong, Robert. With enough of it, money can buy whatever you want. Name one thing that you ever wanted that you couldn't have had if money was no question.'

The doctor's eyes looked fleetingly at Ida. He shrugged. 'World peace? Love? Health? Respect? Shall I go on?'

Gerald laughed. 'I beg to differ...'

Ida intervened. 'Gerald, this conversation is inappropriate. You know money talk bores me.'

'I'm considering taking my knowledge abroad,' Robert said suddenly. 'I haven't decided where, yet. Somewhere far away. Central America, perhaps.'

'Sounds interesting. That part of the world is really opening up,' Gerald said. 'I have a Park Lane office. We must have dinner. You and I can finish our conversation on the merits of wealth and, more importantly, I want to get to know all of Ida's friends. It's the only way I'll learn all her darkest secrets. She's very tight-lipped about such things. She likes to portray herself as sweetness and light but I don't believe it for a second. She can't be as entirely perfect as she makes out.'

'I assure you, she's far from perfect,' the doctor said. He broke into a laugh. 'I'm sorry. I get nervous at parties and make bad jokes. I'm pulling your leg. She has the biggest heart of anyone I know. She'd do anything for anyone. You know that yourself. After all, she was volunteering when you met her.'

Ida blushed. 'You're too kind, Robert.' She turned to Gerald. 'I told you he was a sweetheart.'

Gerald guffawed. 'What she actually said was that you disapprove of our whirlwind romance.'

'You have something of a reputation, Langley. I'm simply looking out for my friend.'

'Looking out for yourself more like, perhaps?'

'Don't be ridiculous. We're friends, and nothing more. My concern is wholly Ida's welfare.'

'Well, I can report first hand. Her welfare is in safe hands.' He squeezed Ida's waist.

'Stop it,' Ida said. 'You're embarrassing poor Robert.'

Robert's face reddened.

'I'm sorry,' said Ida. 'My husband's a little tipsy.'

'Ignore me, Rob. If I've got off on the wrong foot then I'm sorry. I want us to be friends. Truly I do. I'm not only a little drunk, but I'm giddy at having found the love of my life.'

'Excuse me,' Robert said. 'I need some fresh air.' He made for the other side of the room where Margaret Winters was examining a tray of drinks. He took a glass and stood out on the sun terrace.

At the back of the room, Barnes, conferred with Lord Dalton before his lordship addressed the room. 'I'm reliably informed that almost everyone's now here for the first of our celebratory dinners. The only guest missing is my good friend, the acclaimed private detective Henry Fleming, who offers his sincerest apologies. He's running late and will join us shortly. In the meantime, I'd like to invite you all to make your way through to the dining room.'

CHAPTER FOUR

Lord Dalton took his seat at the table. While his focus remained on his guests, he leaned back to listen as Barnes whispered into his ear. 'Would you like us to wait five more minutes before serving dinner, my lord?'

Lord Dalton observed that his guests were all engaged in conversation and appeared content. 'I think that would be appropriate. I know Fleming would want us to continue without him but I think we can hang on a while longer. He's a stickler for punctuality. For him to be late suggests a matter of great importance has arisen and kept him from us.'

'Very good, my lord.' With a discreet gesture Barnes indicated to the footman, Alfie Mason, that he required his assistance in the kitchen. The footman dutifully followed.

Lady Stafford sat beside Lord Dalton at the table, and he felt sure she must have switched places with Sir Peter, who was now next to Ida's attractive young friend, Joyce Toule, who was doing her best to look interested as Sir Peter talked without pause. Peter had somehow invited himself during a meeting to discuss an expedition he had planned. He'd found him rather unpleasant then and his opinion hadn't changed.

Dr Singer was on the other side of Joyce, but seemed unable to get a word in. He'd hoped the two youngsters might find common ground, with them both being friends of Ida.

'Good staff are nearly impossible to come by these days,' said Lady Stafford. She made a show of checking the time on the clock behind Lord Dalton. 'It's nearly half-past and not even a sniff of dinner.'

Lord Dalton smiled apologetically. 'It's entirely my fault. I'd hoped Henry Fleming might have joined us by now. I assure you the first course will be along at any moment.'

'You're also short-staffed.'

He nodded his agreement. 'Barnes and the young footman Alfie are quite excellent. A couple of the kitchen staff are relatively new, but experienced.'

She turned to Vincent Ackerman, who was sitting across from her. 'Did you say something, young man?'

Ackerman looked surprised, his face and ears

instantly pinking. 'I was explaining to the major a little of the history of the London Stock Exchange.'

'Fascinating it is too,' the major said.

'I thought you were supposed to be an accountant. Do you also profess to be an historian?' snapped Lady Stafford.

Gerald spoke up from across the table. 'He's a fine accountant, Auntie. In only six months, he assures me he's saved me a small fortune in taxes and found some sound new investments. You should find time to sit down with him.'

She sighed. 'I've had my man for over fifty years. I won't be changing anything now.' She shook her head. 'And, please, how many more times must I tell you, Gerald? Do *not* call me Auntie. I know you do it only to vex me.'

Gerald tried to hide his smile as he winked at Ackerman.

Lady Stafford lifted her head and spoke authoritatively. 'With the war only just behind us and with Europe far from settled, I'm sorry to say, an experienced money man is essential.'

The major's eyes lit up. 'Mark my words,' he said. 'Something needs to be done, and done now. There are flames still smouldering across Europe, and there are those who wish to fan them. I'm sorry to say further conflict seems inevitable.'

'Surely, it can't happen again,' Ida ventured.

Before the major could build up a head of steam and launch into a lecture, Lord Dalton interrupted. 'No politics at the table, please, Digby. Especially, this being a weekend to mark a special occasion.'

'Of course. My apologies.'

Barnes had quietly shown Fleming into the dining room, where the butler caught his lordship's attention with a subtle cough.

Lord Dalton smiled from ear to ear. 'Our final guest for the weekend, Henry Fleming, has arrived. I'm sure he needs no introduction. If there's anyone who doesn't know him, he's not only my good friend but also the country's finest private detective.'

'Sincere apologies for my tardiness. A small matter of national importance demanded my attention. I hope you'll all forgive the interruption.' He bowed to Lord Dalton and sat down opposite Margaret Winters.

'You're here now. That's the main thing,' said Lord Dalton. 'And, quite by chance, you've arrived at precisely the right moment. Here comes our first course.'

Barnes and Alfie placed soup in front of the guests.

'Sustenance. Finally!' Lady Stafford exclaimed as Barnes presented her with a bowl of thick green liquid. She leaned forward to examine it, lifted a spoonful toward her nose and sniffed gingerly.

'Pea, my lady,' said Barnes.

'I can see that for myself! I may be getting on in years, but I'm not blind. Its ghastly green colour was an instant giveaway.'

'My apologies.' Barnes topped up her wine glass.

'Let's hope it's not cold,' she grumbled out loud for all to hear. Having tried a few mouthfuls, she declared the soup inedible and demanded a glass of sherry to remove the foul taste from her mouth.

'I think it's quite delicious,' Ida remarked. 'Please thank the cook,' she said to Barnes.

Lady Stafford glared venomously.

MARGARET WINTERS FINISHED her soup and turned to Fleming. 'So, you're the great detective I've read about in the newspapers? You're not what I was expecting at all.' He took out a handkerchief and rubbed his nose. Her strong perfume had caused a little discomfort.

From the twinkle in her eye, Fleming understood she was teasing him. Her wine glass was empty. A second glass, a tumbler, was also empty except for ice. As she spoke, he noticed her eyes were on the prowl for the footman, or Barnes, to refill her glass. 'I'm curious to know what you'd imagined?'

'I don't really know?' She tilted her head to get a better look. 'You appear... normal. In some ways, at least. A man who's surprisingly down to earth, able to converse with riff-raff such as myself, yet clearly well-heeled and enjoys fine clothes. Some might consider you handsome, I suppose. I think it's your deep, dark eyes that interest me most. They're alert to their surroundings without making it obvious. I'd wager your instincts have sized us all up already, haven't they?'

'I think I have the measure of those who might be trouble, Mrs Winters.' He raised his eyebrows towards her and laughed.

'You mean me,' she said with a giggle.

'I'm teasing, of course.' Fleming ignored his wine and instead sipped a glass of lemon water. 'In all seriousness, observations can be made, but nothing more.'

'In that case, how do you establish whether someone is guilty of a crime or not? Surely, a great detective has an instinct for such things?'

'Instincts are important and I'll admit I've been blessed in that department. I've also honed many techniques over the years and acquired considerable experience.'

'A life dedicated to your work.' Her eyes met his. 'I read in the newspaper that you're unmarried.'

Fleming placed a hand on the pocket watch in his

waistcoat. He cleared his throat. 'I consider myself married. Though, unfortunately, she and I didn't make it to the altar.'

'I'm sorry. I didn't mean to upset you,' Mrs Winters said.

'It's quite all right. I'm just a little jaded. My work in London has made for a difficult few days, with very little sleep.'

Mrs Winters switched to water.

Ida and Gerald rose, excusing themselves. Ida patting her hair as they left the room.

'I understand from Lord Dalton that your niece, Joyce, has been friends with Ida for many years. You must have known Ida a long time?'

'Joyce is very fond of Ida.'

'I sense some reservation?'

'Ida brings Joyce out of herself. She's a shy girl, often lacking in confidence. Whereas Ida has no trouble landing on her feet.'

'You're clearly very protective of Joyce.'

'I love her like my own.'

There was a moment of silence between them.

'Ida and Gerald appear very happy,' Fleming remarked.

'It almost makes you believe that true love really does exist. That it can overcome any obstacle placed in its way.'

'From what I've heard, Gerald is as besotted with Ida as she with him. I sense though that his godmother doesn't approve of the marriage.'

Ida and Gerald returned. She touched her hair, and Fleming realised she had made some quick adjustments. The happy couple resumed their seats, joking and chatting together.

Lady Stafford couldn't bring herself to look at them. Instead, she spoke to Lord Dalton, who listened politely.

'That old warthog disapproves of day turning to night and night turning to day. As far as I can tell, she doesn't have a good word to say about anyone or anything. Miserable doesn't begin to describe her. How Gerald turned out so well is beyond me. He's impetuous, no doubt, but he's smart as a whip, ambitious, and keen to seize the day.'

'*Carpe diem*,' Fleming said, raising his water in a toast.

Mrs Winters touched her glass to his. 'Seize the day,' she echoed.

'You two appear to be getting on like a house on fire,' said Gerald. He leaned back in his chair so he could see Fleming more easily. 'You be careful, Margaret. If you have a dark secret, this man will uncover it. He's a bloodhound in human form.'

'May I congratulate the pair of you,' said Fleming.

'I have a wedding gift which I'd like to present to you at some point over the weekend.'

'You shouldn't have,' Ida said. 'That's very sweet.'

'I told you, Fleming. She's perfect. If ever a woman was to keep me grounded, and away from my madcap adventures, it's Ida.'

'I hope I'll get to know you better, Ida. Or should I say, Mrs Langley.'

'Ida, please. You're practically family, according to Gerald.'

Fleming smiled proudly. 'If I may say, the two of you look the picture of happiness. After all Gerald's adventures, searching for lost riches, it would seem he's finally discovered a treasure beyond his wildest dreams.'

Gerald beamed from ear to ear. 'You can pack that in right now, you old charmer.' He turned to Ida. 'Though, in truth, he's hit the nail on the head. There I was in Africa searching for diamonds when I stumbled upon my Ida in a nearby village. She was in a spot of bother and I practically had to rescue her and her friends. What are the chances!' He looked into her eyes. 'There and then I knew. I knew with complete certainty that I'd found the finest, rarest, and most precious gem of all.' He turned back to Fleming. 'Henry, I want you to have breakfast with us tomorrow. Spend time with Ida. I want you to know her and look out for her the way you've looked out for me. Would you do that?'

Fleming bowed his head and placed a hand on his heart. 'It would be an honour.'

CHAPTER FIVE

Lord Dalton had breakfasted early and was trout fishing with Major Fielding and Sir Peter. He'd assured Fleming he would be back just after midday and wished to catch up on his week's exploits over lunch.

Having arrived for breakfast and waited several minutes, Fleming wondered whether Gerald and Ida had forgotten their arrangement. As newlyweds, who hadn't known each other very long, he suspected he was not foremost in their minds.

Ida's friend, the young lady, Joyce Toule, was alone at a table. She appeared distracted, staring out through the French doors across the vast estate.

'May I join you, Miss Toule?' Fleming asked.

'Of course, that would be lovely.'

Her glum appearance was instantly transformed

when she smiled. She gestured for him to sit and asked Tilly to bring them both some breakfast tea.

'I understand you're a friend of Gerald's?' Joyce said. Her soft, dark curls bounced as she spoke.

'I knew Gerald's parents, and his father in particular was a good friend. I've known Gerald since he was an infant. At times, I think, he still behaves like one.' Fleming was pleased to have made Joyce laugh. 'Ugly looking baby he was too,' he added.

Joyce laughed even more. 'And now he's all grown up and married.'

'I suspect I'm not the only person who's a little surprised at the speed with which *that* happened.'

Joyce nodded. 'Ida and I always promised we'd be bridesmaids for one another. That's not to say I'm not delighted for them both.'

Fleming agreed. His eyes glanced towards Lady Stafford. He spoke softly. 'The baroness, I suspect, is quite furious. I've done my best to avoid her so far. No doubt she'll attempt to corner me later today when I'm sure to feel the full force of her outrage.'

Joyce giggled again. 'She can be quite fearsome.'

'She's a pussycat. It's just a matter of knowing how to handle her. I'll let you in on a little secret in case you should ever need it.' He reached into his jacket and took out a small white box tied with a blue silk ribbon. 'Inside are sugared almonds. They're her favourite and never fail to put her in a good mood.'

Joyce's eyes shone. 'What a clever idea.'

He slid the box discreetly across the table to Joyce. 'Take it. You never know when it might come in handy.' He patted his jacket pocket. 'I have my own small tin of sweet treats that I carry with me always.'

Joyce put the small gift box in her bag.

'Did you school with Ida?' asked Fleming.

'We've known each other since we were children, but we didn't school together. I was privately educated. My family has money.' She shifted uncomfortably. 'I'm an only child and quite an anxious person. I've always found it hard to make friends. One day I discovered Ida climbing trees near our house and we've been close ever since. She's like the person I wish I could be. Beautiful, confident, glamorous and outgoing. The only thing I had that she didn't was money.'

'Now she has that too,' Fleming observed.

Joyce nodded. 'It was the only thing that differed between us. I used to say to myself that I'd trade all my wealth to be as attractive and carefree as Ida.' She forced a smile. 'Now she's married, I'm back to being alone again. It seems I've come full circle and hardly anything in my life has changed.'

'What's changed is that you're no longer a child. You've grown up and, if I may say so, into a quite lovely young woman.' Fleming noted the arrival of Gerald and Ida, who were engaged in conversation with Margaret Winters. He leaned forward and spoke quickly to Joyce. 'A second piece of advice, if I may?'

Joyce leaned close. 'Of course,' she said conspiratorially.

'The good doctor. Robert Singer, I believe is his name...'

'That's right. He too is a friend of Ida's.'

'I have a feeling he would enjoy your company. An afternoon walk together might be in order. He attempted to speak to you several times last evening but was thwarted by Sir Peter. This morning the doctor has looked this way several times already and I'm sure it's not me he's interested in.'

Joyce touched her neck, which gently prickled with a rush of warmth. She carefully turned in her seat to catch Dr Singer looking her way. He smiled. She smiled back and turned away. 'Do you think so?'

'I would wager a considerable sum that with a little encouragement, he'd summon the courage to speak to you. Men can be shy too.'

Joyce decided she would no longer stay for breakfast. She quickly excused herself and made her way to the sun terrace where she sat reading a book.

Fleming got to his feet and welcomed Ida and Gerald to the breakfast table. Gerald ordered strong coffee, bacon, eggs, and toast, while Ida and Fleming ordered fresh bread rolls and jam.

'It feels like we've spent the entire weekend so far apologising,' Gerald said. 'There isn't anyone I haven't offended by marrying Ida in the way I did. The foolish thing is, we thought it was romantic and everyone would see that.' He drank down a cup of black coffee and then another. 'I might as well hear your honest opinion. Come on, Henry, let's get it out of the way.'

Fleming put down his butter knife and dabbed his mouth with a napkin. 'It matters not what I say or think.' He took Ida's hand. 'You fell in love. The two of you. When this happens, you only have eyes for one another. When you're together, and your heart sings the songs of love, the rest of the world becomes merely background noise. What does it matter what this old man thinks?' Fleming resumed buttering his roll. 'On the other hand,' he said with faux seriousness. 'I would have enjoyed the excuse of buying a new suit and shoes for the occasion. For that, I can never forgive you.'

Ida and Gerald laughed.

'My real concern is Lady Stafford,' said Ida. 'She's taken a real dislike to me.'

'I've spoken to her,' said Gerald, 'but you know how she can be. Stubborn isn't the word for it. She has this bee in her bonnet about Ida only having married me for my money.' He shook his head. 'It's true, Ida hasn't had the privileged background I've had. Yet, we love each other. She refused several times when I proposed. I practically had to beg her before she agreed to marry me.'

'It's true,' said Ida with a fond chuckle. 'Every day in Kenya he came to me and asked for my hand. I thought he was an uncouth, childish nuisance. Certainly not ready for marriage. Eventually, he persuaded me otherwise.'

'What changed?' asked Fleming.

'I'm not sure. One evening at sunset, I realised we'd been talking for hours. The conversation had flowed and we were at ease together. We have the same values, similar goals, and I was suddenly aware there was more to him than I first thought. Of course, it helped that he's passably attractive.'

'Devilishly attractive, you mean.' Gerald nudged her and kissed her cheek. 'Even if I were only passably attractive, you're stuck with me now.'

'Tell me how you met,' asked Fleming.

'It's a story of heroism,' said Gerald.

'I was nursing in a local village when a fight broke out,' said Ida. 'Two villagers were arguing over cattle and it became violent. A group formed, and things were getting out of hand. I suddenly felt quite trapped and vulnerable. Gerald appeared out of nowhere and helped myself, other nurses, and a doctor return to his camp.'

'I'd been out prospecting and was returning for the afternoon,' Gerald said. 'I'd heard about the English working in the nearby village and so dropped by to introduce myself. What luck to bump into the same glorious woman I'd met before at the Southern Summer Ball?'

'Serendipity,' Fleming said. 'A chance event that ends in a happy way.'

'You'll do it then?' said Gerald.

'Do what?' Henry asked, confused.

'You'll speak to Lady Stafford?'

'What?! No. That task is greater than any even the mighty Henry Fleming could undertake.'

'Come on, Henry, you promised my father you'd look out for me. This is one of those moments.'

Fleming gave Gerald a disapproving look. 'That's unfair, young man.'

'Please, Henry,' said Ida. 'It would mean so much to us. To me, her blessing would be the greatest wedding gift of all.'

Fleming sighed but couldn't help but smile. 'Two against one. You've planned this. Gerald, your underhand tactics are quite despicable. You brought Ida here to melt my heart. You're as cunning as they come.'

'Then you'll do it?' asked Gerald.

'Reluctantly, I'll speak on your behalf but, I hasten to add, I can make no promises of success.'

Ida got up and gave Fleming a hug. 'Thank you.'

'Speaking of wedding gifts.' Fleming raised his hand and gestured for their wedding gift to be brought to him. Tilly brought it over. He then presented Gerald and Ida with a small square box. 'Please, open it.'

Ida undid the bow and opened the lid. She lifted out the contents. Uncertain of what their gift was, the pair looked questioningly at each other.

'It's a hip flask,' Fleming explained. 'Your father had it with him when we were together in Italy. Your mother gave it to him before he left England, before they were married, in fact.'

Gerald ran his fingers over a dent. 'This is the flask that saved his life when you were young men.'

'That's right. Your father, he could be hot-headed back then, got into an argument with some local Italian men near Bologna. Suddenly, a bullet came out of nowhere. At the sound of the shot, the men scattered. I then realised your father had been left badly wounded. The bullet had ricocheted off the flask, but he was hurt. I helped him to a medic.'

'You saved his life.'

'The flask did that,' Fleming demurred.

Gerald turned to Ida. 'Fleming carried, and dragged, my father to the nearest hospital.'

'Your father insisted on giving me the flask when we returned to England. He said it would bring me luck, the way it had for him. He believed that because both the hip flask and myself had saved his life, we therefore belonged together. It also meant he should marry your mother because she also saved his life by gifting him the flask in the first place. He said it was fate.'

Ida held Gerald's hand.

'I know it doesn't have inherent value,' Fleming said. 'I hoped, perhaps, it would bring you and Ida luck for your future together. I've wanted to return it to you, Gerald, for a long time. Now seems appropriate. I hope you like it?'

Gerald looked at Fleming with tears in his eyes. 'It's the best wedding gift I could have ever asked for.'

'It's truly thoughtful,' Ida agreed. 'Thank you.'

Gerald rose and shook Fleming's hand. 'You're a good man, Henry.'

DR SINGER JOINED Fleming at the breakfast table just as he was about to rise and leave.

'I'm sorry to bother you,' said Dr Singer.

'Not at all. Please sit. How can I help?'

He hesitated.

'Does your trepidation have anything to do with young Joyce?'

Dr Singer's eyes widened. 'Well, yes. How did you know?'

'I have a nose for such things,' he said with a chuckle.

'Rather than make a complete fool of myself, I wondered whether it would be entirely inappropriate of me to talk to her. Only, she's... and I'm not...'

'I'm not sure I understand.'

'She comes from money. My situation is... but of course, she's...' He looked at Fleming. 'Am I making myself clear?'

'Crystal,' said Fleming. 'Can I assume you're unattached?'

'Yes, of course.'

'You're presumably also a well-educated, professional, interesting, and self-sufficient young man?'

'I'm certainly most of those things. It's that my family...'

'Yes?'

'Well. I'm not from a family with means. My becoming a doctor was something of a miracle. We've also had our fair share of tragedy. My brother had an underlying illness and was in an accident at work that caused the death of another man. I often feel I'm not meant to have happiness. Yet, when I see Joyce I want to speak to her. Find out all there is to know. I've never felt that way before.'

'I can tell you from first-hand experience that feeling that way might only happen once in a lifetime. It could slip through your fingers or be snatched from you in an instant. Don't hesitate. Summon whatever strength you must to seize the moment and talk to her. If you do and it doesn't go well you *might* regret it. If you don't speak to her, when you know you should, I promise you will most *certainly* regret it for the rest of your life.' He tapped the side of his nose. 'I have a feeling that Joyce will welcome the opportunity to have a conversation. In fact, you could well find her alone on the sun terrace at this very moment.' He turned his gaze slightly to where she was sitting.

Dr Singer smiled and took a deep breath. 'Thank you. I'll do it. I'll speak to her.'

'Good man.' Fleming chuckled to himself as he watched the doctor leave the room. He didn't wait to see whether he joined Joyce on the terrace. He knew it was a foregone conclusion.

CHAPTER SIX

Having completed a strenuous walk of the grounds to clear his head Fleming headed back in the direction of Watermead Manor. The iron gate squeaked as he entered the water garden and he noticed Ida sitting alone on the wall of an ornamental pond, the centrepiece of the garden.

'Forgive me. I didn't mean to disturb you,' Fleming said as he turned to retrace his steps.

'It's quite all right. Why don't you join me? I'd welcome the company.' She got to her feet and adjusted her scarf against the light breeze.

'If you're sure,' he said. 'Where's Gerald? He hasn't abandoned you, I hope?'

'He and his accountant are working in Lord Dalton's study. Gerald's been agitated about some financial matter for days now and insisted they discuss it so he and I can enjoy the rest of the weekend. Next week we're expected in Edinburgh for a late summer ball, and I was hoping it would be just the two of us. It seems Ackerman shadows Gerald everywhere he goes. I don't mind the man, but it would be nice to be alone with Gerald for a time.'

'I understand. Though you're married, I imagine you're still getting to know each other. After all, your romance has been, though I dislike the expression, something of a whirlwind.'

Ida took Fleming's arm, and they began walking. 'Do you think I've been awfully foolish?'

'Why would you say that?'

'I love Gerald. I couldn't be happier. Though I worry he's not the settling down type. What if married life makes him unhappy? We could both become utterly miserable.'

They walked in silence for a moment while Fleming considered her question. 'When Gerald was a boy, I would visit him from time to time. As you know, his godmother, Lady Stafford, was his custodian from a young age. She did her best to care for him and she did so in the only way she knew. Even back then, she was quite the disciplinarian. You might say, she ran a tight ship. She was strict with schooling, sporting activities, mealtimes, bedtimes. A lot was expected of the boy. Those traits are now ingrained in him. Gerald has grown into a self-sufficient man who enjoys competing and success.'

'I see that in him. He likes to win at whatever he does.'

'What he missed out on was love. Of course, Lady Stafford loves him in her own way, but it's not the same. No doubt he loves her too, but he didn't get his mother and father's love. After their ship sank, he was all alone in that big house with Lady Stafford, and their many servants, who'd come and go due to her demanding nature.'

'Poor boy.'

'Gerald loves you; I see it in his eyes. If he's having a hard time expressing his feelings, it might be because he needs a little help, and patience. The rest you'll work out together.'

Ida squeezed his arm. 'Gerald said you were a marvel. He was right.'

As they left the water garden and approached the path that ran beside the lake, Sir Peter and Margaret Winters came into view through the rhododendron bushes. Mrs Winters appeared to be extremely cross.

'That's odd,' said Ida. 'Why would Mrs Winters and Sir Peter be arguing? Something must have happened.' She let go of Fleming's arm and picked up her pace. As they rounded the corner, Sir Peter broke off the conversation and walked quickly back towards Watermead Manor.

'What was that about?' asked Ida. 'Are you okay?'

Mrs Winters nodded reassuringly. 'Oh, it was nothing. That man's intolerable.' She looked at Fleming, who was some distance away. 'I don't want to go into detail, but stay away from him. He's nothing but a common conman. I've met his sort before.' She sighed and smiled. 'Now! More importantly, how was your walk?'

'It was lovely and just what I needed.'

'Has Mr Fleming been interrogating you?'

Fleming pretended he hadn't heard.

'Not at all,' said Ida. 'He's been a perfect gentleman, and supportive beyond words.'

'Well, at least someone around here is.' She smiled at him appreciatively. 'It seems to me yours and Gerald's opinion is what counts, and nobody else's.'

Fleming caught up with them and together, the three returned to Watermead.

VINCENT ACKERMAN SAT at a table on the terrace, smoking furiously. His cup of strong tea had gone cold, and on the table beside it lay the briefcase he carried with him everywhere, his elbow resting atop. It was filled with papers, and the year's accounting figures. Rumour had it that on occasion, for safekeeping, Ackerman even slept with the case by his side.

Not wishing to disturb the man, who appeared deep in thought, Fleming pulled out a chair and sat at the next table. As he did so, Ackerman raised a hand and gave a half-smile.

Fleming acknowledged him with a small nod.

No sooner had he sat down though than Ackerman got to his feet and, clutching the case to his chest, scurried away.

Tilly brought Fleming a pot of tea and a slice of warm apple tart. 'Will there be anything else, sir?'

'No, thank you. This tart looks magnificent.'

As he looked up, Fleming observed Tilly's eyes and nose were red and her cheeks flushed. He was certain she'd been crying. 'One moment, please.' He took the small fork and cut the tart. 'Would you be so kind as to try a little piece?'

Tilly was unsure what to make of this strange request.

Fleming pulled out a seat. 'Please, sit for a moment.'

Tilly looked around and, seeing no sign of Barnes, did as she was asked.

Fleming moved the plate towards her. 'Have you tried this tart yourself?'

'No, sir. It's French. Lord Dalton knows a fella that can get his hands on fancy cakes and pastries from Paris. His lordship has a sweet tooth.'

'All these amazing pastries and you've not tried one?'

'No, sir.'

'If you would be so kind,' invited Fleming. He held out the fork. 'I'd like to know whether there is cinnamon in the tart. The French are masters of all manner of culinary delights, and yet I'm a man whose taste palate is quite traditionally English. As a boy, my mother would make an apple dessert but without such exotic spices.'

Tilly sat beside Fleming and took the small forkful. As she tasted the tart her eyes met Fleming's and widened, her face breaking into a smile.

Fleming raised his eyebrows, grinning at her excitement. 'It's good?'

'Wonderful!' agreed Tilly.

'You must try more,' he insisted. 'Is the pastry buttery and light?'

Tilly needed no further encouragement. She tasted a larger piece. With her mouth still full, she nodded. 'Uh-huh.'

'Are the apples creamy and soft?'

'They melt in my mouth.'

'Perfect. And what about the cinnamon? Is there cinnamon?'

'I'm not sure,' admitted Tilly. 'I don't know what cinnamon tastes like.'

The two of them laughed.

'There's a taste that's a little bit like the medicine made with cloves my mother gave me as a young 'un.'

Fleming clapped his hands excitedly. 'Excellent description, young Tilly! That will surely be the cinnamon flavour we're attempting to detect.'

Tilly giggled. She looked at the plate. 'I've eaten it all?'

'On the contrary. There's one mouthful left. You must now eat that and, as you do so, consider everything we've learned. The light buttery pastry, the creamy soft apple, and how the orchestra of flavours come together.'

She chuckled as she devoured the last piece. 'Mm!'

'How was that?'

'Delicious!'

Fleming grinned with pleasure. 'I'm delighted.'

'Would you like me to get you another slice, sir? There are only crumbs left.'

'I'd better not.' He patted his waistline. 'I imagine

there will be a feast this evening at Lord Dalton's dinner.'

'Thank you, Mr Fleming, sir. You've been very kind. I should get back to work.' She took the plate and disappeared into the house.

Fleming poured his tea and smiled to himself. Out of the corner of his eye, he caught Lady Stafford watching him with disapproving eyes from the sitting-room window. He turned away to face the sun. As he sipped the tea, his smile turned to a chuckle.

'MIND IF I JOIN YOU?' Sir Peter said.

'Not at all.' Fleming motioned for him to sit.

Fleming took a small decorative tin from a specially added pocket inside his jacket. The ornate, painted tin had been a gift and he never left home without it. He opened the lid and removed a sugared almond which he popped in his mouth.

'Sweets?' enquired Sir Peter.

'A little indulgence of mine. They help me think. I concentrate on the treat and oftentimes *voila*! An idea forms in my mind.' He offered the tin.

'Not for me.' Sir Peter looked uncomfortable. 'It's been quite an eventful weekend in one way or another.' He pressed his fist against his chest. 'Indigestion,' he explained. 'My doctor prescribes these tablets, but as far as I can tell, they're a waste of time.'

'Really?'

'I'm being a little over-dramatic,' he chuckled. 'They help a little, but when I'm trekking through dense jungle, battling through a blizzard, or in the middle of a raging Atlantic storm, am I really supposed to remember to take a pill?'

Tilly passed him a glass of water.

'Thank you, my dear.' When she was out of earshot, he added. 'Pretty girl that. Though not as lovely as young Joyce. What a delightful young woman *she* is. So interesting as well. It wasn't until I got speaking to her that I realised we had much in common. Admittedly, I'm considerably older, but all the same, I'm looking forward to conversing with her more this evening.' He looked around. 'I can't say I've seen much of her today.'

He examined his two pills, then swallowed them, one after another, washing each one down with water. Speaking louder than Fleming would have liked, he said, 'As for her governess, Mrs Winters – have you encountered the woman? Of course you have. I appear to have got off on the wrong foot with that one. I politely mentioned my interest in young Joyce by enquiring after her position. Not in a direct way, of course; I've only just met the girl. Yet, it was as if I'd woken the Chimera itself. She told me in no uncertain terms that I should stay away from her and her niece.' He swept his thinning hair to one side, his blue eyes squinting at Fleming.

'It would seem the doctor has taken a shine to Joyce. I believe they've taken a boat out on the lake.'

Sir Peter bit his lip thoughtfully. 'Really?'

'I'm afraid so.'

He slumped back in his seat. 'How disappointing. I was feeling quite reinvigorated for a time there. It appears I misread the signals. She's quite wealthy, I believe?'

Fleming frowned. 'Her financial status isn't something I can help you with. As for the signal you may or may not have read, my advice would be to proceed with considerable caution. From one gentleman to another, I'd suggest you're barking up the wrong tree.'

'Do I sense you've had a similar experience with a young woman, Fleming?'

'Personally? No. Those days are long past.'

'Well, I don't plan on giving up without a fight. With any luck I'll be sitting beside her at dinner again this evening, which will give me an opportunity to further my cause.'

'If you feel you must. But never let it be said I didn't warn you.'

'I'll take my chances, old chap. The chase is all part of the fun, wouldn't you say?'

Fleming was about to try a more direct response when Sir Peter jumped to his feet and headed in the direction of Ackerman and Gerald. 'I'll let you know how I get on. However, right now, I've bigger fish to fry.'

CHAPTER SEVEN

When Ida returned to the house, she and Gerald had gone for drinks, and that left Ackerman alone until Sir Peter joined him. Sir Peter's earlier request to discuss his business proposals had been politely rejected but the two men now sat smoking on the front steps of the manor house.

'Look here, I've been associated with many extraordinary adventures and I can tell you that the benefits of investing in any of them have far outweighed the original investment,' said Sir Peter. 'I've just completed a dash across the Gobi desert, and both Colonel Charles Hubert and Lady Clarisse Overton, you've probably heard of them, invested quite considerable sums. They both saw excellent returns, some in ways that can't be measured.'

'That's my problem, you see,' said Ackerman. 'I'm

a numbers man. Dealing in unknowns gives me the heebie-jeebies. And I haven't heard of either Colonel Charles Hubert or Lady Clarisse Overton.'

'Just speak to Gerald, that's all I ask. You're a smart guy. He'll listen to you. The press is going to be all over this and Gerald's name will be associated with it. Mount Everest, the tallest mountain in the world. I'd hate for him to miss out because he didn't think it through, or because he couldn't visualise the potential returns.'

Ackerman flicked away the end of his cigarette. 'You know, we get approached all the time by people with their hands out. I'll speak to him, but you shouldn't hold your breath.'

'Fantastic! That's all I ask. Speak to him or, better still, see if you can arrange a meeting for me to sit down with him. Make it soon though. I have many foreign investors champing at the bit but I'd really love to make this an all-British funded expedition.'

The two men got to their feet. Ackerman walked away and left Sir Peter looking hopeful.

Sitting close to a nearby open window, Fleming had inadvertently caught some of their conversation. He watched as Sir Peter paced back and forth. After a few minutes, he went back into the house.

Fleming turned away from the window. The small sitting room benefited from the warmth of the sun and he returned to his reading: Charles Dickens' *David Copperfield*.

Despite wanting to read, his attention was now drawn to the conversation between Major Fielding and Margaret Winters. He watched the major's eyebrows rise and fall as he listened intently.

'Do you have any children, Major? I only ask because you seem to me like you'd make a wonderful father. I sense underneath your rather stiff exterior hides big old teddy bear.'

The Major chuckled uneasily. 'Well, I don't know about all that teddy bear business, but I'm married and do have one child, a boy. My son, Edward.' He hesitated and chose his words carefully. 'I don't see either of them as much as I'd like and miss them both a great deal.'

'I'm sure you do. The military life can be tough in so many ways. Do you have any pictures of them?'

The major reached into his jacket pocket and pulled out a worn and creased photograph. 'It's not a great likeness. You can't tell in the picture, but they both have the brightest red hair you've ever seen. It's quite something. My boy's the mischievous type, full of smiles and fun. A kind-natured lad. My wife, Fiona, is a true Irish beauty. Skin as pale as snow, eyes as blue as a summer sky and that hair of hers is furnace red.'

He handed her the photograph. 'This was taken quite some time ago.'

Mrs Winters examined the picture. She turned it towards the light of the window. 'What a handsome young man. He has your eyes. And your wife, you're right, she's beautiful.'

'You can see my boy gets his good looks from his mother,' the major said modestly. 'I'll see them again soon enough.'

'It must be difficult being a military man to balance career and family,' said Mrs Winters. 'I'm sure they miss you when you're away.'

The major stiffened his lip. 'How about you, Mrs Winters? Might I ask a little about your situation?'

'There's no mystery about me. I started out as Joyce's governess, and I simply never left. She used to call me auntie as a child, and I suppose that's how I feel.'

'I've observed the bond between you.'

'These days, I'm more a personal assistant and trusted friend all rolled into one.'

'Well I never,' said the major.

Mrs Winters checked the time. 'In fact, I'd better be going. I might be needed. We should continue this conversation later, Major. You're very good company.'

'It'd be a pleasure, Mrs Winters.'

As they parted, Fleming looked up and caught a

glimpse of Lady Stafford talking to Gerald's accountant outside the door. Ackerman had clearly jumped out of the frying pan by escaping Sir Peter and into the fire by running into Lady Stafford, who was now angrily banging her walking stick.

Ackerman shook his head and threw his arms into the air.

Fleming closed his book and, in an attempt to hear the conversation, got to his feet and moved surreptitiously towards the door. Unfortunately, his movement, though careful, was noticed and the couple's conversation ceased. This was all the opportunity Ackerman needed to break away and bound up the stairs, leaving Lady Stafford frustrated.

'Good afternoon, Lady Stafford,' said Fleming in greeting.

'Henry,' Lady Stafford replied stiffly.

'Is everything okay?'

'Quite fine, thank you,'

'It would seem the accountant, Ackerman, is a popular fellow. Though his nerves appear almost completely shredded.'

'I'm not entirely sure he's up to the task of managing the Langley fortune. However, who am I to interfere? Any advice I offer these days to either Gerald or Ackerman is greeted with a mixture of suspicion and contempt.'

'I'm sorry to hear that. It would seem the young no longer value their elders' most valuable asset: their years of accumulated wisdom.'

'I couldn't agree more. You've hit the nail on the head as usual.'

'I'll bid you good afternoon,' said Fleming. 'I think I'll rest before dinner. I understand there will be music this evening.'

'Unfortunately, I've heard the same news, and *modern* music to boot. I'm not entirely certain what Lord Dalton's thinking. It would seem to me he's trying to recapture his lost youth which, I suppose, is only to be expected from men of a certain age.' She pursed her lips, grimacing as though sucking on a lemon.

Fleming opened his mouth, then closed it again.

'What is it, Henry? You look like a gasping fish!'

'Well, I was wondering if we might discuss the surprise wedding at some point over the weekend?'

Lady Stafford eyed him keenly. 'I see Gerald has sent you as a peace envoy. Is he perhaps hoping you might be able to calm the stormy seas between us? Or is it that *she's* charmed you, just as readily as she seduced *him*?'

'I thought we might look at everyone's position and find some middle ground.'

'You disappoint me, Henry,' Lady Stafford

growled. 'I will protect Gerald and his legacy at all costs. Whatever it takes. I'd rather die than sit by and watch the Langley family name besmirched by her. Do you hear me?!' She stamped her cane, then again for good measure, before turning and walking heavily away.

Barnes appeared. 'Everything satisfactory, sir?'

'I've investigated the most testing cases in almost every corner of the world, and yet I find navigating the nuances of family dynamics to be the most challenging of all.'

'Quite so, sir. I find it best to avoid such entanglements wherever possible.' Barnes' friendly eyes appeared sympathetic. 'Would you like something to steady the nerves, sir? A brandy, perhaps?'

'Thank you, Barnes, but I rarely take alcohol.' He gently tapped the side of his head. 'A clear mind at all times is imperative. One never knows when the next challenge might present itself.'

CHAPTER EIGHT

It was a fine late summer evening and the French doors in the drawing room were open on to the sun terrace.

As guests arrived, Barnes explained that pre-dinner drinks were being accompanied by music from a jazz band. On the terrace, the smooth voice of the female singer, elegant in a long, glittering silver gown, sang and swayed to the tempo of the backing musicians. The sound could be heard throughout Watermead Manor, and most of the guests had come down early.

Surprisingly, Lady Stafford insisted on sitting close to the doors. Though wrapped in a thick shawl against what she called a *Siberian chill*, she appeared, for the moment, to be content. Having first scorned the idea of such entertainment, she now watched intently. There even appeared to be the hint of a smile at the corners of her mouth, although Lord Dalton had suggested to Major Fielding that it might be the sun in her eyes, causing her face to contort.

Dressed in a pristine evening suit with a crisp white shirt, Lord Dalton was in fine spirits. Pleased at how well the music had been received, he was in buoyant mood. 'More champagne, Barnes,' he told his butler. Lord Dalton was making his favourite cocktail, the French 75.

He turned to Fleming and spoke close to his ear. 'Now you've had a chance to examine them up close, what do you make of the newlyweds?'

'In what way?'

'You know what I mean. Ida's a fine woman. As Gerald seems to have married her on the spur of the moment, he might just as quickly get bored with married life. I'd hate to think he regrets his decision and breaks her heart. You know the chap. What do you make of it all?'

'I see little that would cause me to intervene, if that's what you're asking. In what little time I've seen them together, they appear very much in love.'

'That's good enough for me, my friend. In that case we should drink to their happiness.' He poured another cocktail. 'I know for a fact that if you had any suspicions, you'd speak to Gerald. I know you've got a soft spot for the lad.'

The two turned at the arrival of the newlyweds.

'Wow!' exclaimed Lord Dalton.

Ida was dressed in a red silk crepe gown with glass bead embroidery, while Gerald sported a fashionably cut midnight-blue suit. The pair barely stopped to talk before moving straight onto the terrace to dance.

Joyce, dressed in white, with feathers in her hair, grabbed the doctor's hand and pulled him after them.

'It would seem Joyce and Dr Singer are getting along,' remarked Fleming.

Lord Dalton nodded and passed Fleming a lime and soda. 'If I had any rhythm at all in my body, I'd be dancing myself.'

'That sounds like a very poor excuse, my friend.' The two men laughed. Fleming took his drink and decided to mingle.

Major Fielding sat in a large chair, smoking his pipe and drumming his hand. His huge eyebrows jumped to the beat of the music, and occasionally he *pom-pom-pommed* along.

Happy to watch from afar, Sir Peter Upton stood at the back of the room, leaning against a side-table.

Vincent Ackerman arrived late. He looked awkward without his briefcase, as though his hands had no place to settle. He headed straight for the bar and helped himself to a large gin.

'Are you a modern music fan?' Mrs Winters asked Fleming.

'I was in New York City not so long ago where I was taken to watch a jazz orchestra. It was quite an eye-opener.'

'Champagne, sir?' Barnes asked. 'Lord Dalton will shortly be proposing a toast to the happy couple.' He held a silver salver full of glasses.

'Perhaps a little,' Fleming said, taking a glass, 'as this is a celebration.'

Mrs Winters drank the remains of hers and exchanged her empty glass for a fresh one. She winked at Fleming. 'I'll take another. As you said, it's a celebration!'

The singer turned to the saxophonist, who played a solo. He was followed by the drummer, who furiously thrashed his drums then slowed the beat, at which point the singer joined in, singing softly. Her voice lilting, expressive, and beautifully timed, she captivated her audience and eventually closed the song to enthusiastic applause. Gerald yipped and whistled, much to Lady Stafford's displeasure.

'How terribly vulgar,' she muttered. 'Yes, please, Barnes, another glass of the cocktail.'

'The French 75, my lady?' He held out the salver.

'Yes, please. Are you certain this is from a different bottle? My last drink was flat and bland.'

'I'm quite certain, my lady. Though if you prefer, there's also champagne and other drinks available.'

'The French 75 will be adequate.'

He handed her the cocktail.

Lord Dalton stopped Barnes and spoke quietly to him. 'If you could ensure dinner is ready, I'll make a short speech and we'll come through to the dining room straight after.'

'Very good, my lord.'

Ting, ting, ting!

Lord Dalton tapped a glass with a silver spoon. He stepped out from behind the drinks bar, where he gathered everyone for his speech. In front of him, a low table was laden with glasses and bottles of wine, champagne and cocktails, as was the sideboard to his left.

'Our quite fabulous musicians are, unfortunately, now leaving us and heading back to London,' Lord Dalton announced.

There were cries of 'Shame!' followed by a loud and appreciative round of applause.

'However, on a positive note, this gives me an opportunity to say a few words about our guests of honour, Ida and Gerald.'

Dr Singer raised his glass and drank it down in one. 'What a terrific idea! However, why don't we hear from the lucky man himself first? I'm sure Gerald would like to say a few words. Let's have a speech from him.'

'Absolutely, I love the sound of my own voice,' laughed Gerald.

'A drink first!' declared Dr Singer. 'We need to be able to toast the marriage properly.'

Ida wobbled on her feet and knocked a bottle of champagne off the sideboard, the fizz spraying everywhere. 'I'm so sorry. All the dancing has made my head spin.' She knelt down to pick up the bottle, but Tilly got there first. 'I'm so sorry,' she repeated to the maid.

Dr Singer turned to the sideboard and placed two champagne cocktails on a silver salver. 'This'll soon set you straight,' he said to Ida.

'Or make me worse,' she joked.

He placed two more cocktails on the tray. 'Nonsense! Us dancers need some refreshment. Here we go, my friends!'

Both Ida and Joyce took a glass, as did Gerald. Dr Singer was about to take his when Gerald swiped it from the tray. He winked cheekily at the doctor, drank it down, and laughed. 'I hope you don't mind, old boy!'

'Of course not, it's your party,' said the doctor with a laugh as he took another cocktail from the sideboard. 'I plan on getting roaring drunk too!'

'Does everyone have a full glass?' asked Lord Dalton.

Using her cane, Lady Stafford struggled to her feet and held hers aloft. 'I have mine,' she declared.

Sir Peter picked up a fresh drink and stepped away from the bar, allowing Mrs Winters to add more ice to her glass. Fleming handed a brandy to Major Fielding, who was not a fan of anything with fizz.

Dr Singer raised his cocktail. 'Down the hatch!' He took a long, satisfying gulp.

'I'm parched from all the dancing, and from simply being happier than any man alive,' said Gerald. He followed Dr Singer and drank down his cocktail in one go. He then grabbed two more from a low table in the middle of the room and passed one to Dr Singer. The two men drank simultaneously. 'Ah! That's much better!'

'I suppose we ought to leave some for the rest of the guests,' joked the doctor. 'You're supposed to be making a speech, not starting a drinking competition.'

There was a ripple of laughter.

'A little Dutch courage before the speech, perhaps?' Fleming said.

Gerald winked. 'You know me too well, Henry. I'm not one for speeches, but my new wife appears to have quite transformed me. I feel invincible.' He grabbed Ida's waist and squeezed her.

Suddenly, with a gasp, Gerald swayed and staggered forward. His eyes widened and a surprised look crossed his face. 'Good gracious, it seems the champagne has gone to my head.'

Ida laughed. 'Too much alcohol on an empty stomach, my dear?'

The whole room laughed.

Gerald stumbled to one knee, his hands clawing at his throat as he desperately tried to draw breath.

'He can't breathe!' screamed Ida.

Gerald slumped to the floor, his body convulsing.

Dr Singer sprang into action and was instantly at Gerald's side. He loosened his shirt collar and attempted to ease his breathing. 'Stand back, everyone!'

After a few moments of frantic activity, he checked for a pulse. Fleming knelt opposite Dr Singer and they exchanged a knowing look.

The doctor turned to Ida. 'I'm so very sorry,' he said. 'There's nothing more I can do.'

Ida fell into a dead faint.

Mrs Winters let out a low, pitiful moan.

Joyce, who appeared perfectly calm and in control, rushed to help Ida.

Lord Dalton dashed into the hallway, yelling for Barnes.

Fleming rose to his feet and looked purposefully around the room, staring at every face in turn. When he spoke his voice was grave. 'I believe I can say with certainty that Gerald has been poisoned.'

'*Poisoned?*' queried Major Fielding.

'Yes, Major. Or, to put it more bluntly, he was murdered.'

Lord Dalton reappeared, he looked distraught. 'That's preposterous!' he insisted. 'Are you saying someone's tampered with our drinks?'

'That's precisely what I'm saying.'

Sir Peter stepped away from the drinks bar and thrust his hands into his pockets.

Dr Singer was quite pale. His attention had turned from Gerald to the empty glasses around the room. 'What if we've all been...' he faltered, swaying back and forth.

'Are you okay?' asked Mrs Winters.

The doctor, gasping and shaking now, stumbled and fell onto the side-table, sending glasses flying. He veered towards the centre of the room and collapsed onto the low table, before finishing face down on the floor.

'WELL, HE'S DEAD ALL RIGHT,' Inspector Carp announced. He scratched his head and looked at the body. 'Poisoned, you say? Are you certain?'

'Quite certain. Your pathologist will be able to confirm my suspicions, but from the manner of his death, I would suggest the poison is most likely strychnine. It somehow found its way into his drink.'

On hearing this, Lord Dalton stared at his glass of brandy and placed it gingerly down. 'Are we in danger of further poisoning?'

'I think not. Though all glasses and bottles must be examined for traces of the poison. In particular his glass.'

'Which was his?' asked Inspector Carp.

Lord Dalton shrugged. 'It could be any of them. It could even be one of the smashed glasses.'

'A dead end then?'

'Perhaps not,' Fleming said. He got down on his hands and knees to retrieve a champagne flute which had rolled under the table. Holding it carefully with a handkerchief, he held it up to the light. 'There are no traces of lipstick, suggesting it belonged to a gentleman. This is very likely the glass he was holding when he collapsed.'

'I'll get it examined immediately.'

'Very good, Inspector.'

'How's the doctor?' asked Inspector Carp.

'He has a few cuts and bruises but he'll be fine. His was most likely an emotional collapse from the shock,' said Fleming.

'He wasn't poisoned?'

'No. Fortunately, he's made an excellent recovery.'

'Gave us all the fright of our lives, that's for sure,' said Lord Dalton.

Inspector Carp looked relieved. 'One murder is quite enough.'

'What's your course of action from here, Inspector?' asked Fleming.

'Well, for a start, I'm going to need statements from everyone.'

'I'll inform them, and make the appropriate arrangements. When would you like to begin?' asked Lord Dalton.

Carp checked his watch. 'I'll make a start immediately.'

'Are you sure that's a good idea?' asked Lord Dalton. 'The women are quite distraught. Ida, especially. Lady Stafford has taken a sedative and Joyce appears quite detached and fearful.'

'I suppose it could wait until the morning. I'm in need of a good night's sleep myself. I'd just got off the boat from Jersey when I received notice I was to come straight here.'

'We're obliged that you came as promptly as you did, Inspector. I look forward to working with you again,' said Fleming.

Carp smoothed his moustache. 'I've a feeling there's going to be a lot to work out, and with the sudden death of a person of Gerald Langley's station, I suppose it would make sense to have an extra pair of hands.'

'I quite agree,' Lord Dalton concurred. 'Fleming here has a personal interest in finding the culprit. He's practically part of the Langley family. He was also in the room at the time of the incident and has met all the guests. This investigation simply couldn't proceed as effectively without him.'

Inspector Carp looked browbeaten. 'In that case,' he sighed, 'we should resume in the morning. Of course, it goes without saying, nobody must leave Watermead Manor. Tell the guests to try to get a good night's sleep. Tomorrow will be a long day.'

Inspector Carp was shown out by Barnes. 'Shall we say nine a.m. sharp, Inspector?'

'That'll do nicely,' agreed Carp. He turned up his collar against the drizzling rain and walked towards his car.

'Would the library suffice, sir?' called Barnes.

Inspector Carp looked up at Watermead Manor, and all its many windows. 'As long as that's no inconvenience.'

'Very good, sir. We'll see you in the morning.'

CHAPTER NINE

'The glass had no traces of the poison?' repeated Fleming. 'Are you sure?'

Inspector Carp nodded. 'They tested all the glasses for strychnine and found nothing. Although the pathologist confirms Mr Langley died from strychnine poisoning.'

'How extraordinary. I shall give it some thought.'

Three armchairs had been placed in the middle of the room, two on one side of a small table, and one on the other.

Barnes entered the library. 'Is everything to your satisfaction, sirs?'

'Ideal, thank you, Barnes,' Fleming confirmed.

'Start sending them in if you would,' Inspector Carp said.

'Very good, sir.' The butler paused before exiting. 'In any particular order?'

Inspector Carp looked questioningly at Fleming.

'Ladies first, perhaps? It would seem improper to keep poor Ida waiting longer than is necessary.'

Carp scratched his chin. 'Ladies first. Naturally.' He waved a hurrying hand towards Barnes, who nodded agreeably.

'Of course, sir.' He left the library and a few moments later Ida Langley appeared.

Carp waited for her to settle in the armchair.

She was red in the face and carried a handkerchief. With dignity, she held her head high and, despite her frailty, she looked both men in the eye.

'Mrs Langley, I'm terribly sorry to be asking questions at a time like this, but there's a job to be done, and it falls on me to investigate the circumstances surrounding your husband's death. Overnight, we established that Gerald was indeed poisoned. As Fleming surmised, the substance in question was strychnine.'

Ida sobbed and clasped her hands. 'But how?'

'That's something we're looking into.'

Ida looked at Fleming. 'You were right, last night, when you said poison killed him.'

'I'm so sorry,' Fleming said.

Her eyes moved back to the inspector. 'I understand perfectly what you must do, and I wish to assist with your enquiry in any way I can.'

Carp tapped a pencil on his notebook. 'I'm not someone who likes to beat about the bush, Mrs Langley.'

'Neither am I, Inspector.'

'Very well.' Carp thumbed his moustache. 'In that case, I'd like to address the most obvious and irrefutable fact first.'

'Which is?' She gave Carp a stern look.

Carp looked at Fleming for support but realising he was on his own at this point, charged on. 'You stand to inherit a large fortune now your husband's dead.'

'Yes,' Ida agreed.

Carp swallowed hard. 'It therefore occurs to me that...'

'That I have the most to gain from his death.'

'Precisely.'

'You should remember though, that I've also lost the most, Inspector. You see, Gerald and I were very much in love. You've heard of that notion, I suppose? When every waking moment is filled with thinking about that one special person, and you can no longer imagine a future without them. That someone with whom you hope to start a family, and grow old and grey with. One unique person you'd give your own life

to save? Have you experienced any of that, Inspector?'
Ida glared coldly at Carp.

The inspector cleared his throat and referred back
to his notes; opened and closed his mouth a few times.
'You're clearly very upset,' he ventured at last. 'I think
it's best we come back to you when you've had a little
more time.'

'How *very* considerate.' Ida stood. 'When all you
have is a hammer, Inspector, everything looks like a
nail.'

Carp waited for Ida to leave before letting out a
huge sigh of relief. 'In retrospect, Fleming, starting
with the women might have been a mistake. Questioning the men first might have been a better idea.'
Then, seeming perplexed, he shook his head. 'Do you
have any idea what she meant by my having a hammer
and nails?'

JOYCE TOULE and Mrs Winters arrived together.
Fleming sprang to his feet and pulled over another
armchair.

'Thank you,' they said in unison.

Fleming turned to Carp. 'Would you like me to
assist?'

All eyes were on the inspector who chewed his

pencil while he considered the question. He spoke quietly to Fleming from behind a hand. 'Go ahead, it'll give me a chance to pick up on anything that sounds suspicious.'

'As you wish.' He turned to Mrs Winters. 'I apologise if some of my questions appear a little intrusive. Sadly, we find ourselves in this unhappy place and we must all journey together to uncover the truth. I hope you'll forgive any directness.'

'We're keen to help,' the two women agreed.

'Very good. Firstly, Mrs Winters, what were your feelings about Ida marrying Gerald?'

Mrs Winters softly patted her pleated skirt with a gloved hand. 'I'll admit I wasn't at all surprised.'

'Why's that?'

'Ida's always been an ambitious young woman.'

'The truth is, Ida's always been determined to climb the social ladder? Isn't that so?'

Carp momentarily looked up from his notes and raised his eyebrows.

'I wouldn't have said it quite like that myself. Ida comes from a poor background. She met Joyce, and has used her ever since.'

'Do you see it like that, Joyce?'

Joyce gave a gentle shrug. 'I don't think she means any harm. After all, don't we all want to feel comfortable and secure? If Gerald had shown me the same interest he showed her, then it might have been me he'd married. Would I then be under the same scrutiny?'

'It's you he should have married,' said Mrs Winters. 'The difference being that while she threw herself at him, you behaved like a lady.'

Joyce huffed. 'I'm quite plain and she's beautiful. That's the truth of the matter. It seems to me that her success at marrying exceptionally well is being held against her.'

'You make a valid point,' said Fleming. 'I'm merely attempting to eliminate her from the investigation, but it seems clear she has the most to gain from Gerald's death.'

'A woman from Ida's background has fewer options than a man to better herself. Maybe his murder has nothing to do with gain. It might be that someone hated him, or was jealous, or was seeking revenge?'

'You have a very astute mind and make a sound point.'

'I'm merely looking after my friend.'

'Yet, it's undeniable you were a stepping stone towards Gerald. She used your connections and friendship to give her credibility.'

'Perhaps,' said Joyce. 'We're well off, not rich like Lord Dalton or Gerald Langley. We certainly don't have that sort of money. But I'm very comfortable and have good connections. I'm certain Ida recognised that.'

'I love you dearly, Joyce, but you've always been blind to her manipulation,' said Mrs Winters. 'She uses people. Do you really believe her meeting Gerald in Africa happened by chance? Somehow, she orchestrated it. Both of them are in Africa. The same place, at the same time? Who financed her little trip? That's what I'd like to know.'

'She loved Gerald,' Joyce insisted. 'He loved her.'

'And after the shortest courtship in history, she marries one the most eligible bachelors in England. Then just as quickly, he's dead. You don't see that as odd?'

Joyce began to cry.

'Joyce, my dear,' Fleming said. 'You know Ida better than anybody. Were there any indications that she was unhappy?'

'None at all.' She dabbed her eyes with a handkerchief. 'Despite what Auntie says, I know Ida wouldn't harm a fly. I'm aware she used me to improve her position. I allowed it. I needed a friend, and she always looked out for me. In many ways, I used her too.'

'One last thing,' Fleming said. 'Are you aware of anyone with malice towards any of the guests attending this weekend's celebrations?'

They both shook their head. 'Why would you ask that?' Mrs Winters enquired.

'We can't rule out the possibility that Gerald wasn't, in fact, the intended target. That perhaps he inadvertently drank poison meant for someone else.'

Carp almost dropped his pencil at this revelation, then hastily echoed Fleming. 'Quite. The intended target could have been anyone in the room. Let's bear that in mind.'

LADY MARY STAFFORD entered using a walking stick. Barnes was keen to assist and offered a steadying hand.

'If you're daring to infer that I need help from an underling, you're *very* much mistaken! Now get out of my way,' she raged.

Barnes bowed and stepped aside. 'Of course, your ladyship.' He gently closed the door behind her.

'Why on earth a lady of my years is made to struggle all this way is beyond comprehension. Any gentleman worth his salt would have come to *me*,' she complained pettishly. 'Instead, I'm forced to traipse the halls like a dizzy scullery maid who doesn't have the sense she was born with.'

After making a great show of getting comfortable

in her armchair, she scowled at the two men. 'Let's get on with it then, I've things to do!'

Carp cleared his throat and busied himself with his notepad and pencil.

Before saying anything, Fleming reached into his pocket and took out a small decorative tin. He lifted the lid and held it in front of Lady Stafford.

Her ladyship put on her spectacles and peered inside. Fleming could see a childlike gleam in her eyes. She took out a sugared almond and closely examined the sweet treat before popping it into her mouth. She did not bite, she did not suck, but simply let it rest upon her tongue.

Notebook and pencil forgotten for the moment, Inspector Carp appeared completely mesmerised by this ritual.

'Lady Stafford, I'm sorry for your loss. You and I have known each other for a long, long time and I know Gerald was like a son to you. I therefore apologise for the inconvenience caused by asking you to attend this investigative formality, which we must carry out with urgency for Gerald's sake.'

Lady Stafford appeared to have softened and, having taken off her glasses, gently nodded her appreciation. 'Please, continue, Henry.' She stared gimlet-eyed at Inspector Carp. 'And you are...?'

'Inspector Carp, your ladyship.'

'Oh yes,' she sniffed dismissively.

'It would be fair to say that Gerald's estate is considerable and that as his godmother you've resided at the family residence, Chippingwood Hall, since the death of his parents,' said Fleming.

'In my opinion, for Gerald to grow up in his family home is what his mother and father would have wanted and so, in answer to your question, yes, I've lived at Chippingwood Hall since their untimely death.'

'How has your relationship been with Gerald since you discovered his marriage to Ida?'

'Perfectly fine.'

'No disagreements?'

'No more than usual. He's always been a wilful young man. He can be hot-headed. You know that as well as I.'

'He knew his own mind, that's for certain, your ladyship,' Fleming agreed.

'What were the arrangements upon his return from Africa? Were Gerald and Ida living at Chipping-wood Hall?'

'For heaven's sake! You know all this, Henry. If you have a question to which you *don't* know the answer, please have the courtesy just to ask it. Don't take me for a fool, or continue this tip-toeing around. It's far too tedious.'

Fleming rubbed the pocket watch in his waistcoat with his thumb. 'I understand you were given an ultimatum by Gerald? Either accept Ida, or leave. Is this true?'

'*Gerald* would never have forced me to leave Chippingwood Hall.'

'Meaning?'

'It was *her*. She put ideas into his head. She wanted me gone, preferably feet first. Failing that, then out of his life completely.' Lady Stafford curled her lip and looked away. 'There's something about her I instantly disliked. My instincts have guided me well over the years and I saw no reason to mistrust them on this occasion, either. It would seem they were right. My boy is dead.' She let out the slightest whimper before reining in her emotions. 'I loved Gerald like he was my own.'

'Thank you, your ladyship, that's all for now.'

MAJOR FIELDING SIPPED brandy and sucked on his pipe. 'Had I wanted to kill the lad I'd have shot him straight between the eyes,' he proclaimed. 'Poison is for cowards, women and spies.'

'Thank you for that clarification,' Fleming said. He

opened a window to allow in some fresh air then returned to his seat.

'You're most welcome.'

'Though in my experience that's not always true.'

The major released a large cloud of smoke. 'All this talk of strychnine is utter nonsense in my opinion.'

'You have your own theory, then?'

'Of course I do. You don't rise through the ranks of the British army by following the herd, believe you me. Africa! That's what killed him.'

'Africa?' Carp repeated, puzzled.

The major frowned. His bushy eyebrows appeared almost to cover his eyes completely. 'I've seen it myself first hand, and not just on that continent. Apparently fit men can suddenly be taken ill for any number of reasons. Mosquitoes, poor sanitation, contaminated water or food, snake bites, you name it. Probably brought something back with him.'

Inspector Carp folded his arms. 'Our pathologist confirmed he was poisoned here in Watermead Manor with strychnine.'

'We'll have to agree to disagree on that point, Inspector.' The major rolled his glass thoughtfully around in his hand, examining the golden liquid.

Carp stubbornly shook his head. 'It's a fact—'

Fleming interjected. 'How well did you know Gerald?'

'I didn't know the chap at all. Never met him until this weekend.'

'You therefore know Ida?'

'Lovely girl, but never laid eyes on her till Friday.'

'You don't know either of them?' Fleming said.

'Correct.'

'Then why are you here?' Inspector Carp asked bluntly.

'I asked myself the same question only this morning. Lord Dalton invited me for a spot of trout fishing this weekend and here I am.'

'He invited you this weekend, despite the celebration?'

'Correct. The fish aren't bothered by what's going on in the manor house, so I suppose this weekend's as good as any other.' He chuckled to himself and finished the last of his brandy.

CHAPTER TEN

Vincent Ackerman hadn't brushed his hair, and his shirt was partially unbuttoned. He glanced nervously around the library. 'Can you repeat the question?'

Inspector Carp leaned forward to get a better look at him. 'You controlled Gerald Langley's finances? Correct?'

'It's a little more complicated than that. But in simple terms, I suppose I did.'

'Did you or didn't you oversee every penny that came and went?'

'To some degree, yes, I did. He had considerable wealth and many interests. Only recently he's invested in a steel mill in the United States, a beef farm here in England, a diamond mine in South Africa. Then there are all his late father's investments.'

'Overseeing all that is a considerable task for just one man,' Fleming suggested.

'Not really. I'm good with numbers. May I get a brandy?' He looked around for Barnes, but he was nowhere to be seen. Spotting a decanter on a side-table, he got up and poured himself a large measure. He cautiously sniffed the golden liquid before drinking.

Inspector Carp and Fleming exchanged glances. 'Are you all right?' Carp asked. 'You appear very on edge?'

Ackerman drained the glass, then poured another. He wiped his mouth with the back of his hand and returned to his seat. 'My employer was murdered yesterday. That'll mean a mountain of paperwork. I have to get back to it. There's lots to be done.'

'We're nearly finished, for the moment,' said Fleming. 'Was Gerald a good employer?'

Ackerman frowned and anxiously rubbed the top of his leg. 'I don't understand the question.'

'I'm sorry. Let me rephrase it. Did you enjoy working for Mr Langley?'

'I suppose I did. Mr Langley himself wasn't very interested in the finances. He left it all to me. I did my best. He enjoyed other pursuits, making deals, adventures abroad, acquiring fine goods and luxury items. Of late he was buying a lot of gifts for Ida but he rarely kept the receipts. That made things very difficult for me. I tried hard to balance the books but he made it very tricky.' The brandy seemed to have had a calming effect. 'I never gave much thought to whether I enjoyed it or not. It's my job.'

'Would you mind if, maybe later, we looked at some of the paperwork?' Fleming asked.

Ackerman drained his second glass of brandy. He shrugged. 'I suppose that'll be okay. There's not a lot to see for the untrained eye. It probably won't make sense. But you're welcome to look.'

'Thank you, Mr Ackerman, that'll be all for now.'

Ackerman handed Inspector Carp his empty glass and left the library. Carp stared at it in disbelief. 'What an infernal cheek! Does he think I'm one of the staff now?'

SIR PETER UPTON flicked his cigarette into the fireplace. His hands were large and rough; his face tanned, deeply lined and leathery. Fleming noticed that one of Sir Peter's thumb nails was missing.

'Gerald and I were considering an expedition,' he explained. 'You see, like him, I'm something of an explorer. There's a big world out there. Plenty of scope to make a name for oneself. The only problem is that the window of opportunity is closing fast. Right now, there's huge interest in climbing Mount Everest and I'm keen to put a team together to make the first successful ascent. I thought Gerald might be interested in a jolly to the top.'

'That's why you're here this weekend?' Carp asked.

'I wouldn't want to intrude on the man's celebration, but I thought perhaps there might be an occasion to mention the idea in passing.'

'I was unaware Gerald had participated in expeditions of this nature. Prospecting in remote countries, yes, but climbing mountains, trekking through jungles or crossing deserts, no,' said Fleming.

'The fact of the matter is, I fully expected Gerald to turn me down on any actual participation. Especially being newly married, and the nonsense that goes with it.' He chuckled. 'These jaunts are a costly exercise and it takes investors to fund them. Gerald's a good sport. We've talked about financing in the past, and I thought he might support our cause. Unfortunately, it would seem my timing was a little off. Unless the new Mrs Langley is keen on such things, and happy to spring us more than a few shillings.'

Fleming frowned. 'You appear to have little regard for the fact a man has died.'

'That's a little unkind. You don't make history

without determination and a will of iron. I was gambling on his helping. The fact he's died could put back months of planning. Someone else could reach the summit before us.' He lit another cigarette. 'I'm merely being straight with you.'

'Yet, I'm left wondering whether you are, in fact, "being straight" with me.'

BARNES OPENED the door to the library and from his seat, Fleming could see Dr Singer whispering to Joyce Toule along the hall. The pair were holding hands. Upon seeing him watching, Joyce broke away and disappeared from view.

Beside him, Carp was crossing out and re-writing notes in his little book. 'You know, it could have been one of the staff that did it. We should speak to them too.'

'If you like,' said Fleming absently. He watched Dr Singer approach and take his seat. He reclined and made himself comfortable. He crossed his legs and watched Carp with amusement.

'Joyce is worried about me. In case you're wondering what we were talking about,' said Dr Singer to Fleming. 'I don't look well enough to be up and about, apparently.'

'You do look rather pasty,' said Carp, looking up from his notebook. 'We'll keep this brief.'

Dr Singer opened his cigarette case and put a cigarette to his lips. 'You'd think I'd know better,' he said. He struck a match, lit the cigarette and with a trembling hand dropped it into Ackerman's empty glass, which rested on the table between them. 'I'd all but given up, but this awful business has me smoking like a train.'

'You're a friend of Ida's, I understand?' began Inspector Carp.

'That's right. We go back a few years.'

'Was it ever any more than that?'

'I'll admit, there was a time in my life when I wished there had been more, but Ida would never have settled for someone like me.'

'How do you mean?'

'I'm sure she won't mind my saying. If she were here in this room I'd say it to her face. She always dreamed big. Her beauty, grace, and brains meant she would never have to settle for the likes of me. I'm distinctly average. So, in answer to your question we're just friends.' He forced a smile.

'Did that make you jealous?'

'Of Gerald?' he laughed. 'Jealous enough to murder him?' He laughed even louder. 'Inspector, is that what you think? I murdered him because I was jealous of his marrying Ida?'

'Did you?'

'That's ludicrous. I have a life in London. I'm flat out as a doctor. I certainly don't have time to worry about what Ida's doing. Until this weekend, I haven't seen her in months, in fact, it might even be longer than that.'

'You must have known Joyce Toule before this weekend? She too was a friend of Ida's. They were inseparable from what we've heard.'

'That's the thing about Ida. She keeps her life private. She also keeps her friends apart. It's like she has several personas and we're all pawns that get moved around on her own private chessboard. She was the Queen, Gerald became the King. I was perhaps a lowly pawn, maybe a knight or a bishop, but certainly not a rook.'

'What did you make of Gerald?' Inspector Carp asked.

'I only met him briefly. He seemed a decent enough chap. I'd hoped we'd be friends.'

'You hadn't ever met Gerald before this weekend?'

He shook his head. 'No. I received a letter out of the blue informing me of their marriage. It didn't surprise me; that's typical Ida. Then a telegram arrived inviting me to this weekend. I came along as her friend and, naturally, I was curious to meet Gerald.' The doctor began to tremble.

Fleming frowned. 'Are you okay, Doctor?'

Dr Singer put out his cigarette. 'I'm still a little under the weather. I'm tired. I can't say I slept particularly well.'

'We can leave it there,' said Carp. 'If we have any more questions, we'll come and find you.'

As he opened the door, Joyce was waiting. She put an arm around him and guided him to the stairs.

'I've offered poor Ida my lakeside house in Italy for as long as she wishes, once this investigation is over, of course. She can come and go as she pleases. It's warm there this time of year, and away from it all. When news gets out of her husband's death, the press will no doubt begin hounding her. It's the least I can do. The poor girl's distraught beyond words. Of course, she's putting on a brave face.'

'I could do with a holiday myself!' Carp said.

'We'll have to see what we can do once this sorry saga is over, Inspector,' Lord Dalton said.

'Much obliged, my lord,' said Carp.

Fleming gave him a sharp look, which Carp took to mean that his comment had been highly inappropriate.

'You mentioned the cocktail glasses, tumblers and champagne flutes, Henry,' said Lord Dalton.

'I wondered which of the staff handled them.'

'Tricky one that, but the last people would have been Barnes, the new housemaid, Tilly Caster, and the footman, Alfred Mason. They were the only staff serving the drinks on the terrace. The others were preparing dinner, of course.'

Carp wrote down the names.

'They were pouring and handing out drinks, and I had a go at some cocktails, but everyone in the room was milling around, so anyone could have tampered with the glass. That's the terrifying thing about all this. Just about anyone could have done it. Equally, any one of us could have been poisoned.'

'He's right, you know,' said Carp. He turned to Fleming. 'The way you've described it to me, the room was full and guests were not only being served drinks, but were making their own. Anyone could have poisoned Mr Langley's glass. If indeed, he was the intended target. There are also the musicians, who are on their way back to London.'

'It's not the musicians,' Fleming snapped. 'This was personal.'

'Even so, I feel I must question everyone. One or more of them may perhaps have seen or heard something suspicious as they were packing up and preparing to leave.'

'Quite so,' Lord Dalton agreed.

Fleming sat quietly for a moment, impatiently tapping his finger on the table. 'There's something I'm missing.'

Carp got to his feet and turned to Lord Dalton. 'If you'd be so kind, I could do with the details of the musicians. I really feel I need to interview them, if only to leave no stone unturned.'

'If you speak to Barnes, he'll gladly oblige.'

Carp looked at Fleming, who had taken out his pocket watch. Inside, he thought he caught a glimpse of a photograph, but he couldn't be sure. 'I'll head to London then and leave you to speak to the staff.'

Fleming nodded absently. 'Good idea,' he mumbled.

Inspector Carp and Lord Dalton left him to his thoughts.

A few minutes later Fleming opened the library door and stepped out into the hallway.

'I need to inspect all the guest rooms, immediately,' he said to Barnes, who happened to be passing.

'Immediately, sir?'

'Yes, please.' He placed a hand on Barnes' arm. 'Also, and this is most important, nobody is to return to their room until my search is over. Do you understand?'

'Clear as crystal, sir. I'll see to it personally.' He proudly stuck out his chin and threw his shoulders back. 'Which room would you like to start with?'

'It doesn't matter so long as I see them all.'

'Very good, sir. Follow me.'

At a quick march, the two men started up the sweeping staircase.

CHAPTER ELEVEN

Barnes knocked on the door of Vincent Ackerman's room. Hearing no response, he unlocked it and entered. Fleming followed closely behind.

'As instructed, I'll ask all the guests to remain downstairs while you conduct your... inspection, sir.'

Barnes remained by the door. 'I'll unlock all the other rooms and return downstairs. Will you be needing me for anything else?'

Fleming shook his head. 'You've been most helpful.'

Lord Dalton appeared at the threshold. 'Mind if I join you?'

'Not at all,' said Fleming.

'I've always wanted to try my hand at detective

work.' He opened a wardrobe and peered inside. 'What are we looking for, Henry?'

'Anything that appears out of place. You'll know it when you see it.'

The way Ackerman had left his room appeared less orderly than Fleming had imagined it would be. Wardrobe doors had been left open. Clothes spilled out of drawers. Shoes were in disarray beside an open suitcase.

'Not the tidiest of fellows, is he?' said Fleming.

'I had expected neatness and order.'

Lord Dalton pulled open the curtains and let in some air.

Fleming crouched down to examine the fireplace, which was warm but not burning. With a fire iron, he poked around.

'Have you found something?' asked Lord Dalton.

Fleming picked out a badly charred scrap of paper. He took it to the window to read. 'Interesting.'

'Is it a clue?' Lord Dalton enquired excitedly.

'It may be nothing. It's pages from a ledger. It would seem the fastidious accountant is keen to obscure certain aspects of Gerald's finances.'

'Surely, there must be some explanation.'

'Whether that explanation is forthcoming, only time will tell. I'll speak to him again in due course.

Now we must examine the next room.' Fleming marched on, followed amiably by Lord Dalton.

By late afternoon, Fleming and Lord Dalton had discovered little else of interest. They approached Dr Singer's room when, to their surprise, he came out.

The startled doctor spun around. 'I know I'm not supposed to be here. However, Lady Stafford's nerves are on edge. I was fetching a tonic for her.' He showed them a small bottle. 'I didn't think you'd mind.'

Fleming held out his hand. 'If you'd be so kind,' he said.

'Of course.'

Fleming closely examined the bottle. He removed the lid and cautiously sniffed. 'Lavender?'

'It's all perfectly safe,' the doctor said. 'Just a mixture of natural herbs that has a calming effect.'

Satisfied, he handed the bottle back.

The doctor stepped aside and allowed the two men into his room. 'If there's anything in particular you're looking for, perhaps I can help?'

'If you would be so kind as to return to the others, my examination will be over shortly.'

Fleming waited for the doctor to depart before commencing his search.

'What do you make of that?' Lord Dalton asked.

'The good doctor is certainly full of surprises.'

'He deliberately ignored your request to remain downstairs.'

'We can only assume he's keen to put his patients first.' Fleming examined the doctor's medical bag, which sat on a dresser beside a large window.

Lord Dalton was on his hands and knees, peering under the bed. As he climbed to his feet, he watched as Fleming stopped his search of the medical bag. His attention turned to something else. He was examining the surface upon which the bag sat. As Lord Dalton approached, Fleming put out a hand. 'Don't come any closer, Anthony.'

'Good heavens, what is it, Henry?'

'Granules of powder.' He tutted at himself. 'I almost missed it.'

Lord Dalton watched as Fleming further examined the carved edge of the rosewood dresser.

'Strychnine?'

'It's impossible to tell. But we must proceed with caution. In small doses, a doctor might prescribe such pills for low mood. However, larger doses usually prove fatal.'

'It could simply be make-up powder,' observed Lord Dalton.

'I agree,' said Fleming. 'I'll make sure it's examined by Inspector Carp's toxicologist.' Fleming took an envelope from a bureau and, with a pen, nudged a sample of the powder inside. Folding the envelope, he placed it in his pocket, then returned to examining the doctor's medical bag. He pulled out all the equipment and medicines. 'It's as I suspected.'

'You found strychnine pills?'

Fleming shook his head. 'No strychnine pills. Things are rarely that simple, my friend.'

'What I don't understand is why the doctor would want to kill Gerald. It makes no sense.'

'On that point, I must agree. There's also the possibility another guest has secretly entered his room.'

'I hadn't considered that.'

'At this moment in time, we'll keep our little discovery to ourselves.'

'You have my word, Henry.'

There was a knock at the door and Barnes appeared. 'My lord, I'm sorry to interrupt, but unfortunately, this matter can't wait.'

'What is it, Barnes?'

'It's the young maid, Tilly, my lord. She's been taken poorly.'

Fleming grabbed the doctor's medical bag. 'Let's not waste a second. Lead the way.'

Dr Singer held Tilly's hand. 'How are you feeling, young lady?'

The maid took deep breaths. 'Much better now, thank you, Doctor.' He took her pulse once more.

A small group, including Joyce, Mrs Winters, and Lady Stafford, having heard the calls for help, had gathered in the dining room. Alfie Mason, the young footman, stood beside Fleming, frantically biting his thumb nail. 'Tilly and I had been moving a small table. When we'd finished, she said she felt dizzy and went white as a sheet. Her eyes were staring, but it was like she couldn't see me. Then she fell into my arms. I called for help, and Mr Barnes came running. Has Tilly been poisoned, Doctor? Please tell me she'll be okay.'

Dr Singer got to his feet and Alfie took his place holding her hand.

'I shall need to examine her further, though I feel certain she's not been poisoned. In fact, she's in rude health, but needs to take things a little easier for the time being. She should avoid strenuous work, such as lifting. At least for a while.'

The doctor glanced at Fleming, who immediately understood his meaning.

'I'll look after Tilly,' said the doctor. 'Perhaps Joyce could assist?'

'Of course.' Joyce took Tilly's arm and helped her up.

'Thank you, Doctor,' said Tilly. 'You've been so kind.'

'You're most welcome. And I don't want you to worry.'

Joyce took Tilly's hand. 'Why don't you show the doctor and myself to your room? He can examine you there.'

'Come on, Mr Mason, let's get back to work,' said Barnes. 'Tilly will be just fine.'

The young lad followed Barnes but repeatedly turned his head to look back at Tilly as they left the room.

'But I can't be,' insisted Tilly.

'It'll be fine,' said Joyce.

Tilly and Joyce sat on the edge of the bed. Dr Singer packed away his things into his medical bag.

'No. It won't,' said Tilly. 'You don't understand. I'm a maid. I'll lose my job.'

Tilly looked at Joyce as if for reassurance.

'Does the father know?' asked Dr Singer.

'No. And I can't tell him. We'll both be out on our ear.'

'He works at Watermead Manor?' the doctor asked.

Tilly hesitated and then nodded.

'It's the young footman, isn't it?' said Joyce.

'We're in love. Alfie loves me.'

Joyce smiled sympathetically and squeezed Tilly's hand. 'I'll speak to Lord Dalton. He's a good man, he'll understand.'

'You can't do that,' insisted Tilly. 'I need to keep it a secret. At least until I know what I'm going to do.' She looked imploringly at Joyce and the doctor.

'Of course,' Dr Singer said. 'I won't say a word. However, if you start feeling unwell again, I need you to speak to me, or the local doctor.'

She nodded appreciatively. 'Thank you. I'd better get back to work. Otherwise Barnes'll boil me alive.' She scurried off.

'I feel I should help the poor girl,' said Joyce. 'It all seems so unfair.'

'Unfortunately, there's little that can be done. The girl's been foolish.'

Joyce frowned. '*She's* been foolish? What about the young man's involvement?'

'I'm sorry. I didn't mean it quite the way it sounded.' He looked at Joyce fondly. 'My apologies.'

'Apology accepted.' She gave him a peck on the cheek.

'What was that for?'

'For being so gentle with Tilly.' She chuckled. 'And for making me feel happy. You're good company.'

Dr Singer smiled. He took Joyce's hand. 'I wondered, if perhaps, once this sorry business is behind us, we might see each other again. My parents own a little house in Devon. It's not much, but it's right by the sea. We could get to know each other better. Mrs Winters would be welcome.'

'That sounds lovely. I'll think about it,' said Joyce, smiling coyly. 'We'd better get back to the others.'

CHAPTER TWELVE

Lord Dalton discovered Ida alone down by the boating lake. She looked like she'd been crying. 'I wanted to see how you are?' he said. 'Awful question, I know. I can only imagine how wretched you must feel. I suppose I'm really asking if there's anything you need?'

'I think I'm still in a state of disbelief.'

Lord Dalton sat on the other end of the long bench and looked across the still water. 'I'm sure I've told you this before, but this spot, where we're sitting, was one of my late wife's favourite places. Anne and I would sit together on a summer's evening and talk. She enjoyed the conversation. Well, I say conversation, but it was often quite one-sided.' He chuckled at the memory. 'I enjoyed hearing her thoughts on all manner of subjects. She was a very smart woman. Far cleverer than me. She was always keen on reading about advances in medicine, science and technology. It always brought a smile to my face, seeing how enthusiastic she got when explaining something she'd recently read up on. She could talk for hours.'

Ida took his arm, and they began walking back to the house. 'You've been so kind. Barnes, too, has been an absolute wonder. So incredibly attentive, I can only assume that was at your behest.'

'I was fond of Gerald. Though I only met him briefly, he seemed like a decent chap. I only wish you'd spoken to me before marrying in Africa.'

'Africa seems a lifetime ago now. I can't thank you enough for all you did for me. If it hadn't been for you, I would never have had the opportunity.'

'It was the least I could do. You told me it was your ambition to go there, and I had the money and the contacts. It was easy for me to arrange your passage. You did so much for Anne during her sickness. Like our very own Florence Nightingale, you nursed her, and befriended her.'

'I'm no nurse, that's for sure, but caring for her was easy. As was being her friend.'

'I'll be eternally grateful for all you did. I praise the day Dr Singer recommended you during our trip to Harley Street.'

'He's a good man.'

He cleared his throat. 'It's hard to believe it has almost been a year since Anne passed.'

Ida squeezed his arm. 'It seems we've both endured unimaginable heartbreak.'

'Yes,' said Lord Dalton. They walked in silence awhile. 'I don't know what your plans are for the future, but you're welcome to stay at Watermead Manor for as long as you wish. Also, the invitation to visit the house in Italy still stands. It might do you good to get away.'

'That's very kind, Lord Dalton, but as soon as I can, I must return to Chippingwood Hall to sort Gerald's affairs.'

'I understand. Remember, I'm on hand should you run into any difficulties. A word of unsolicited advice?'

'Of course.'

'Make friends with Lady Stafford. She can either be your ally or your adversary. I'd suggest the former. I'd also keep that accountant Ackerman on a tight leash.'

Ida chuckled. She put her head on his shoulder. 'I love the way you look out for me. But I'm a big girl. I'll be just fine.'

'I hope so. You're going to have leeches coming for you now you've inherited Gerald's fortune.'

'If I need any help, I promise I'll come running.'

He gently patted her hand. 'That's all I ask.'

Having gained his lordship's permission, Fleming tried the door handle to his bedroom. *Do what you must, my friend. I've nothing to hide from you. I never lock my room,* he'd said.

Fleming twisted the handle, and the door opened. When he heard footsteps behind him he stepped quickly inside, then turned and caught a glimpse of a figure. He moved swiftly back along the hallway but as he reached the stairs could see nobody. He sniffed the air. There was a faint, fragrant smell. It seemed familiar, but at that moment he couldn't place it.

Inside Lord Dalton's room, he picked up the same fragrance he'd noticed in the hallway.

He went to the window and opened it. Keeping himself out of view, he stood and looked out across the vast lawns and gardens to the lake. Down below, on the terrace, indistinct voices caught his attention. Sir Peter and Major Fielding, no doubt engaged in another of their fierce debates.

Dr Singer sat alone reading and smoking a cigarette. In the distance, Lord Dalton was returning, arm in arm with Ida. As they approached, he noted that they disengaged and walked separately. Fleming sighed with exasperation at the behaviour of his good friend.

Mrs Winters appeared on the terrace carrying two shawls and she passed one to Joyce as she approached. He watched as the two women wrapped themselves for comfort against the breeze and began to chat.

He carefully inspected the contents of drawers and a wardrobe. On the small writing bureau he scrutinised papers. Other than correspondence between himself and Ida, inviting her and Gerald to Watermead, he found little of interest.

Having seen enough, he went to leave the room. As he grasped the door handle, a glint of something caught his eye on the floor beside him. Hardly visible behind a rosewood cabinet was a cocktail glass. Fleming stooped down and carefully picked it up. Upon examination, the decoration on the glass became apparent. The gold design was the same as on the glass Ida had drunk from, and also Gerald at the time of the poisoning. He carefully wrapped the glass in his handkerchief and was about to return downstairs when he decided to re-examine Major Fielding's room.

He opened the door and looked around. He knew what he was looking for but it was a matter of deciding where it might be kept. The room was as neat and tidy as he expected it to be. The only tell-tale sign of something out of place was the untucked sheet at the end of the bed.

Fleming lifted the heavy mattress and reached

under. He immediately felt what he was searching for. A small pistol. He carefully removed the item and examined it. He took a moment, wondering what to do. Eventually, he decided he had no choice. He lifted the mattress once again and returned the pistol to where he had found it.

Fleming went from room to room. To and fro, back and forth. Examining and re-examining until he was satisfied.

IN THE DINING ROOM, high tea was being served. Seeing Lady Stafford already seated, Fleming sat beside her. Her smile was more of a grimace.

'I'm not sure how I'm supposed to have an appetite, but one must soldier on.'

Fleming took a piece of Victoria sponge cake and a cup of tea. 'My apologies for having spoken out of turn previously. I hadn't meant to interfere or upset you. Gerald's hope had been for you all to get along. I was fulfilling his wishes.'

'Ever the diplomat, aren't you, Henry?' She cut her scone and popped a piece into her mouth. 'I tolerated the vixen in the henhouse and look what happened.'

'It might prove difficult if fences can't be mended,

so to speak. After all, Chippingwood Hall belongs to Ida now.'

'I would sooner bed down with the cattle on the estate than sleep under the same roof as her.' She met his eyes and Fleming could see she meant it. 'I'll be contacting my solicitor at Hugo & Hawes and contesting the will. Of that, you can be *most* certain.'

'Naturally, you must do what you think is right, Lady Stafford.'

She got to her feet. 'I've lost any appetite I might have had. Good day, Henry. I must take my rest.'

Leaning on her cane, she pushed between Dr Singer and Major Fielding who had just arrived. The pair jumped aside to allow her past.

'Was it something I said?' asked the doctor jokingly.

'I confess, it was my own foolishness that caused her departure,' Fleming said.

Seeing Vincent Ackerman on the terrace, Fleming also excused himself.

'I HAVE LOTS TO DO. We can talk later,' suggested Vincent Ackerman. He made to scuttle away.

Fleming placed a firm hand on his arm. 'I'd prefer we spoke now. If you don't mind?'

Ackerman's ears pinked. 'If the matter's pressing, then I'd be happy to assist.'

'Why don't we take a stroll and step away from prying eyes?' suggested Fleming.

Ackerman looked at the tall French doors that opened onto the terrace where he observed Sir Peter Upton watching him. 'Good idea,' he agreed.

The stable block behind the main house was empty and private. Lady Dalton had been a keen rider but, after her passing, Lord Dalton had been at a loss as to what to do with the horses. Not being much of a rider himself, he had little interest in them and, as they weren't suitable for working the land, they were sold.

'I wish to ask you about Gerald's accounts,' said Fleming.

Ackerman's eyes couldn't seem to settle. 'I'm still working on them. I've been left with it all to sort out.'

'I'm tired of all the games, Mr Ackerman. I know you've been stealing from Gerald.'

'That's absurd...'

Fleming cut him off. 'Allow me to finish,' he said. 'With his death, you're free to cover your tracks. His unexpected marriage to Ida meant there would no doubt be a review of his finances. I know from Ida that she's keen to be involved in all aspects of the running of Chippingwood Hall, which would include the finances. I'm also aware Lady Stafford has made certain demands upon you.'

'She insisted on seeing the accounts when she heard of Gerald's marriage, and several times since.'

'You're under immense pressure not only to please everyone but also to hide your misappropriation of funds. Gerald's death gives you some time to conduct your cover-up, but not much. I found fragments of burned ledger pages in the hearth in your room.'

Before his legs gave way beneath him, Ackerman sat on the stables' stone mounting block. He ran a shaky hand through his hair. 'He never noticed. I thought a little here and there wouldn't hurt. I borrowed his money to finance investments for myself. After all, I was increasing his fortune each year. I got greedy. My investments were going well, so I decided to get ambitious. I started taking more and investing more. Then, I lost a large sum in a deal that went south.' He looked ashamed. 'I replaced my lost investment with more of his money. Then, I borrowed even more and lost again. Now, there's a sizeable hole in his fortune that I've been trying to replace ever since.'

Fleming's eyes narrowed. 'The question I keep asking myself is: how far would you go to hide your deception?'

'What do you mean?'

'Did Gerald find out and so you had no choice but to murder him?'

'Murder? No! You don't understand the situation at all.' Ackerman looked at Fleming with fear in his eyes. 'There's something I need to tell you.'

'Go on,' encouraged Fleming.

'I was in the study when I overheard a conversation from the next room. I was working, and only half-listening. There was part of the conversation that only made sense once Gerald died.'

'Did you tell anyone?'

'I spoke to—'

'Mr Fleming! Mr Fleming!' From around the corner, Tilly came running. 'Mr Fleming,' she panted.

'Calm yourself, Tilly. You shouldn't be exerting yourself like this. Breathe slowly,' demanded Fleming.

Tilly did as she was told. When she'd caught her breath she said, 'I was passing Ida, Mrs Langley, I mean, on the stairs when she collapsed. She's awfully unwell. I was told to fetch you straight away.'

'Of course, I'll come immediately,' said Fleming. He turned to Ackerman. 'You and I are by no means finished. We'll resume this conversation.'

Ackerman nodded, looking pale. As Fleming and Tilly ran back to the manor house, he put his head in his hands.

CHAPTER THIRTEEN

By the time Fleming and Tilly reached the stairs where Ida had taken ill, Dr Singer had moved her to her room. Tilly returned to her duties.

'Dr Singer is with her,' said Lady Stafford. 'She seems to have been taking this whole grieving-widow performance too far. The girl appears to faint at the drop of a hat.'

'Excuse my saying, Lady Stafford, but it's not really our place to say how deeply the young woman's hurting. She's bereaved and, judging from the few times I've spoken with her, quite a sensitive soul. She and Gerald were deeply in love and the shock is no doubt tremendous.' He placed a caring hand on her arm. 'You, too, are hurting. I know it. Don't allow your dislike of their marriage to cloud your fond memories of the young man you raised to become a fine and honourable gentleman.'

Lady Stafford puffed and pouted. 'Perhaps – though I very much doubt it – I'm being a little harsh on the girl. It's all been a shock and I'll admit I'm finding it hard to think with any clarity at the moment.' She put an embroidered handkerchief to her nose. 'I shall need a few moments alone before dinner.'

'Of course, Lady Stafford. Remember, I'm here for you, always.'

'Thank you, Henry. As ever, you're a comfort.'

Fleming gave a little bow. 'My pleasure.'

'THE CONVERSATION IS a little subdued this evening, don't you think, Sir Peter?' Major Fielding took a large bite of his pork chop and helped it down with a hefty gulp of Lord Dalton's claret. 'It's as if we're lost behind enemy lines and the rations are low. It's times like these we need to dig in and fight on.'

Sir Peter shook his head. 'The guest of honour's dead, Digby, you old fool. That'll put a dampener on any party.'

The major grumbled to himself but said nothing further.

'The weather looks like it might turn to rain

tomorrow,' Lord Dalton said in an attempt to rally a conversation.

'It certainly looks that way,' Sir Peter agreed. 'Weather-wise, it's been an odd summer.'

The major joined in. 'I think you're right, Lord Dalton, we should expect rain. It's been rather close of late, and a storm will clear the air. It'll be most welcome.'

Lady Stafford tutted and put down her knife and fork with a clatter. 'Is that *really* all we have to talk about? While a murderer lurks among us.'

Vincent Ackerman and Mrs Winters hadn't arrived for the meal. Ida was to eat in her room with Dr Singer. Joyce had offered to keep her company, but Dr Singer turned her down. Having given Ida a relaxant, he thought it best he stayed with her for a little while.

Dr Singer's rejection had caused Joyce to feel rather low. 'I can't face food. I'm sorry,' she said, pushing her salmon aside.

'You must eat,' said Sir Peter. 'It's important to keep your strength up.'

'Is that so?' she retorted snippily. 'Thank you, but if I need your opinion, I'll ask for it.'

Sir Peter looked taken aback. 'I'm sorry if I offended you.'

'Well, that's a start, I suppose. Though I don't for

one moment believe you *are* sorry,' she added. 'Frankly, your whole demeanour offends me.'

Sir Peter straightened his poorly presented tie. 'As I've said, if I've spoken out of turn or done something to upset you, of course I apologise. My being here isn't by choice, y'know. I'm stuck here at Watermead just like the rest of you until this thing's over.'

Joyce was about to respond when there was a blood curdling scream from outside. 'Where's Mrs Winters?' she gasped.

'Good God! That came from the direction of the stables,' cried Lord Dalton.

Major Fielding who had immediately jumped to attention, now wasted no time, quick-marching through the house at surprising speed, the other guests following behind.

Joyce ran to Mrs Winters, whom they discovered, white as a sheet, clinging to a stable door. She raised a shaky hand and pointed. 'There, beside the mounting block,' she half-whispered. 'It's the accountant, Ackerman.'

Fleming had been looking for Ackerman to continue their conversation, and he stepped forward just as Dr Singer arrived, panting heavily. 'What's happened? I heard the scream from Ida's room. It was so loud it woke her.'

Vincent Ackerman lay face down in a pool of

blood. A gash to the back of his head all too evident. An iron fire-poker lay on the ground beside him.

Dr Singer checked for a pulse but shook his head. 'It's no use. His skull's been cracked wide open.'

'Has he been murdered?' asked Sir Peter rather stupidly.

'Unless he bashed himself over the head, it certainly looks that way,' said Lady Stafford sarcastically. She had been the last to arrive, and now leaned on her walking stick peering at the prostrate body with seeming interest.

Fleming took out a silk handkerchief, picked up the fire-poker and examined it closely. 'Do you recognise this?' he asked Lord Dalton.

'It's from the library,' said Lord Dalton, pointing out the unusual handle.

'Who on earth would do such a thing?' asked Major Fielding. 'Ackerman seemed a bit tightly wound but a decent enough chap.'

'Someone wanted to silence Mr Ackerman,' said Fleming. 'He must have seen something, or had information that the killer wants held from the investigation.'

'The real question is who among us had the opportunity to murder poor Mr Ackerman?' wondered Joyce.

'It could have been anyone,' said Major Fielding.

'Of course, bashing a chap over the back of the old noggin isn't very sporting so that rules me out.'

'Well, it wasn't me,' Lady Stafford declared. 'I could hardly have done something so violent.' She grimaced at the very notion. 'I can barely walk these days, let alone crack someone with a poker.' She waved her walking stick and wobbled dramatically to demonstrate the point.

Major Fielding scratched his chin. 'The odd thing is, he asked me for advice not long ago. He told me he'd overheard a conversation while working in the study adjacent to the library. At first it hadn't meant much to him and it wasn't until after Gerald's death that its relevance became clear. Unfortunately, he wouldn't tell me who it was he'd overheard, or what was said.'

Fleming frowned. 'I believe he was about to tell me what he'd heard when, unfortunately, we were interrupted.'

The major nodded. 'Sadly, the lad might have taken the key to this whole affair with him to the grave.'

'It would seem there was an opportunity for several of us to have committed this crime. I left him quite well, suggesting somebody was aware of our conversation, and silenced him shortly thereafter. The only question that remains is motive. Who could benefit from his death?'

LATER IN THE EVENING, Major Fielding joined Fleming in the library. The major drank a large brandy while Henry sipped chamomile tea and pressed him for more information about his conversation with Ackerman and what the accountant had overheard.

'You're an odd bird, Fleming,' he observed, while filling his tobacco pipe. 'I can't work you out. I've had many types under my command over the years and I usually have the measure of a man in no time at all. You, I can't fathom.'

'I'm not a complicated man,' said Fleming placidly.

'There it is,' the major said. 'Of course you're a complicated man. You must be to do what you do.'

'On the contrary. I enjoy my roses, my books, English tea at breakfast and chamomile tea in the evening. My cottage and its grounds on a summer's day is the place I dream of when I'm away, which of late has been far too often. I enjoy walks with my dog, Skip, who, due to my repeated absences, has become more my housekeeper's best friend than my own.'

'What of your investigations? Where do they fit in?'

Fleming smiled. 'For me, solving the puzzle is as vital as breathing.'

'And what of your latest puzzle? You no doubt

have your theories as to what's behind it all?' The major lit a match. He held the flame to the tobacco, puffing a few times until he was sure he had a good burn going.

'Until the death of Mr Ackerman, I was convinced I understood the case. However, this new development has my mind in a whirl.'

The library door opened and in stepped Inspector Carp. 'There you are, Fleming,' he said. 'No sooner do I arrive back from London than another body turns up.'

'Indeed,' said Fleming. 'You interviewed the musicians?'

'They're a funny lot, but I don't see any of them as the killing type.' He perched on the sideboard and folded his arms. He used his thumb to point. 'With Lord Dalton's permission, I've spoken to the other guests and, while the investigation's ongoing, they've agreed to stay a few more days. I assured them the matter can be cleared up quickly.' He looked between Major Fielding and Fleming.

The major took the pipe from his mouth and raised his huge eyebrows. 'I've nowhere to be in a hurry, and I'm quite keen to see how all this unfolds. I'm enjoying my front-row seat.'

Fleming sighed. 'We shall have to work fast. Their patience will wear thin very quickly.'

'That's settled then,' said Carp, hopping off the sideboard. 'Right! There's a belly-busting wedge of beefsteak pie downstairs that the cook's set aside with my name on it. I tell you, Fleming, that's one fine woman and if there were no Mrs Carp, I'd—'

Fleming coughed warningly and Carp subsided.

'Well, er, yes,' he harrumphed. 'I'll catch up with you later, then. I'm off to feed my face. I'm starving!'

'I'll come with you. The brandy in my glass appears to have evaporated,' joked Major Fielding. 'And I'm of a mind to get myself outside another slice of cook's delicious apple pie, while there's still some left!'

As Carp and the major turned to leave the room, Fleming's lips twitched, his brown eyes twinkling with amusement.

JOYCE CAUGHT up with Lord Dalton as he was discussing an additional greenhouse with the head gardener. She hovered while the two men finished their conversation.

'I'm sorry to intrude,' said Joyce.

'Not at all, it's lovely to see you.'

She peered inside the greenhouse.

'The work of the estate must continue unabated.

It's mainly salad and fruit inside that one,' he said. 'However, we're discussing trying out more tropical varieties. Hence my meeting this morning.'

'I once grew a pineapple in our greenhouse,' said Joyce. 'I read about it so gave it a go. It was one of my few experiments that actually worked.'

The two began walking through the vegetable gardens. As they strolled, Lord Dalton detailed the produce they grew for the kitchen, the running of the manor and the recent demand for agricultural land.

'You've surprised me, Joyce,' said Lord Dalton.

'In what way?'

'Your interest and knowledge of managing an estate.'

'I was never that interested in many of the things I was expected to be. I preferred to be outside and more hands-on. It didn't necessarily please my mother and though my father pretended to disapprove, he loved having me around.'

'I'm sure he did,' said Lord Dalton. 'What about Mrs Winters? What did she make of it all?'

'When she realised she couldn't mould me the way my mother intended, she encouraged me to be myself. And here I am. All grown up and very capable.'

Lord Dalton chuckled.

'There's something I need to discuss with you,' said Joyce.

'And what's that?'

She hesitated. Knowing it wasn't her place to say, and that once the genie was out of the bottle it couldn't be put back in. 'It's about Tilly, your maid.'

Lord Dalton frowned. 'Tilly? What about her? She hasn't been taken ill again, I hope?'

'Nothing like that.'

'Has she said or done something to upset you? She hasn't been with us long, but I'd hoped Barnes would have kept an eye on her.'

'It's a... delicate matter,' said Joyce. 'I'm hoping you'll be understanding.'

'What is it?'

Joyce placed a hand on his arm and they stopped walking. 'She's... pregnant.'

'She's what?!'

Joyce looked concerned. 'Don't be angry.'

He shook his head. 'I'm not angry. I'm shocked. Who's the father?'

'It's young Alfie, the footman.'

Lord Dalton sucked his teeth. The pair continued walking. 'How did you find out? Did she share this news with you?'

'It's why she fainted. Lord Dalton, the young girl's terrified you're going to let her go and I'm worried she might do something silly. You will talk to her, won't you? Perhaps reassure her she won't lose her job?'

'Well, I don't see how she can continue in service *and* bring up a baby. I shall have to think about it.'

'She's unmarried and pregnant. If she can't stay on here, what will she do?'

'She must have family. Surely, they can help?'

'I don't know. Please don't tell her I told you. I promised her I wouldn't. I feel she needs help.'

Lord Dalton fell silent. 'I'll talk to the girl. I'm not sure yet what can be done, or how she can continue in service. On the other hand, I'm not inclined to leave her destitute.'

CHAPTER FOURTEEN

Arriving in the dining room, Ida was surprised to see Fleming had already breakfasted. He stood as she approached him.

'Please, there's no need to stand. I see you're an early bird, like me.'

'With such troubles upon us, I find it hard to sleep,' he said. 'If I may say, you're looking well this morning. How are you?'

'The sedative Dr Singer gave me helped considerably. I was able to sleep soundly.' She sat down next to Fleming. 'Such terrible news about Ackerman. Do you have any idea what happened?'

'It would seem he was silenced.'

'Good heavens. Do you think he knew something of Gerald's death?'

'That's what I've been sitting here contemplating.'

Barnes brought Ida tea and toast.

'Thank you, Barnes,' she said. 'That'll be all.'

Lady Stafford arrived next and, to Fleming's surprise, sat down on the opposite side of the table to Ida. She attempted a smile. 'Good morning, my dear. How are you feeling?'

'Much better, thank you.'

Lady Stafford smiled at Barnes as he placed a cup of tea in front of her. 'Thank you, Barnes. That looks perfect.'

Fleming was taken aback by this new Lady Stafford.

'I was wondering if we might talk later today?' said Lady Stafford to Ida.

'But of course. What about?'

Lady Stafford shifted uneasily in her seat. She glanced at Fleming and then back at Ida. 'It's a little delicate. I'd hoped you and I might speak privately.'

'I see. Are you free after breakfast? We could walk down to the boathouse, if you feel up to it?'

'That would be ideal. I'm more than a little tired of being cooped up.'

As Margaret Winters and Sir Peter arrived for breakfast, Fleming made his excuses. In the hallway he met Lord Dalton. 'I have some errands to run today, Anthony, and I wondered whether your chauffeur would take me to town?'

'But of course.'

'Excellent. I'll be ready in about half an hour. I shouldn't be long, but I must send some urgent letters.'

'I can arrange for those to be posted for you, Henry. There's really no need for you to go all that way.'

Fleming lowered his voice. 'Between you and me, I'm also collecting some confidential letters that could help with the investigation.' He tapped the side of his nose.

Lord Dalton caught his meaning. 'I see. I'll have Taylor bring the motorcar round.'

IDA AND LADY STAFFORD sat beneath an awning in front of the boathouse. From their vantage point, they could make out Lord Dalton's open top Bentley heading down the long driveway.

'That's Henry Fleming in the back, isn't it?' said Ida.

'It's hard to say. My eyes aren't what they used to be.'

'It is, you know,' said Ida, squinting. 'I wonder what he's up to?'

'I really have no idea. Despite all the years I've

known the man, he remains an enigma to me. Quite unfathomable, one might say.'

Lady Stafford was holding Ida's hand as though they'd been lifelong friends. 'I know we didn't get off to the best of starts,' ventured Lady Stafford. 'I'll admit to having been over-protective of Gerald, however, I hope we can become friends. I know it's what he would have wanted. If something good can come from his death, I hope it could be that.'

'I'd like that more than anything,' said Ida. 'Gerald spoke of you fondly. He'd want us to get along.'

'I agree,' said Lady Stafford. 'I suppose we should try to get the ledgers and other important papers from Vincent Ackerman's room. I mean, we don't want them falling into the wrong hands or vanishing completely. I shudder to think what might happen if Inspector Carp got hold of them. You know how diabolical the police can be in such matters. If you like, I'll ask Barnes to collect them and bring them to me for safe keeping. I can then arrange for my accountants to bring everything up to date.'

Ida was silent for a moment, shrewdly eyeing Lady Stafford. Having withdrawn her hand, she said, 'I rather think it would be more appropriate, if it all came to me.'

'Of course, but—'

'Chippingwood Hall is, after all, my responsibility now.'

'I assumed that being so... grief-stricken you might not want to be burdened with such matters. I have a very loyal accountancy firm, and legal team, who can safeguard your best interests.'

'*My* best interests? Is that really what this conversation's about?'

'Of course,' said Lady Stafford. 'After all, you're family now.'

'I think perhaps you're looking out for yourself. Maybe hoping that in amongst Ackerman's papers is a will, or some other loophole by which you can declare the wedding null and void, or at the very least ensure I'm side-lined in some way.'

Lady Stafford tried to look hurt, but made a poor show of it. 'I'd hoped we could see eye to eye on this matter.'

'I see perfectly what you're up to. I thought this morning we might have a chance. Instead, it seems you've only one agenda and that's to have me stripped of my rights to the estate and Gerald's fortune.' She got to her feet. 'You're not to be trusted. I see that now. I'm legally Gerald's wife and everything will come to *me*. Once that happens, I want you gone from my life and that includes Chippingwood Hall. I want you out of there! You're no longer welcome.'

'You can't do that! Chippingwood Hall is my home. It's where I raised Gerald.'

'Gerald's gone. There's nothing left for you now.' She turned and walked away. Over her shoulder she said, 'I'll get Barnes to send someone for you. I'd hate for you to fall and hurt yourself, even someone as cold and conniving as you.'

'WOULD you please come in and shut the door behind you?' said Lord Dalton.

'Yes, my lord,' said Tilly. As the maid entered the study, she discovered Alfie already waiting. Joyce stood in front of a large window, flanked by Barnes, who stood stiffly, showing no emotion.

Lord Dalton perched on the edge of his great oak desk. 'Sit down, you two. I need to have a word.'

Tilly and Alfie looked at each other then did as instructed.

'Joyce here has brought to my attention a situation I should have been made aware of before now,' he said. 'I know she promised you she wouldn't say anything, Tilly, but I want you to know she only has your best interests at heart. So would either of you like to start?'

Alfie hung his head.

Tilly sat up straight. 'My lord, I'm not sure what you're referring to?'

Lord Dalton folded his arms. 'The pair of you know exactly what I'm talking about. I hope you're not going to make me spell it out. I simply need to know if it's true.'

Tilly put a hand to her belly.

'Well, is it?' he repeated.

'I'm still very capable,' insisted Tilly. 'I won't let it affect my duties.' She glanced at Joyce, who nodded encouragingly.

'I should think not,' said Lord Dalton. 'Alfie. What do you have to say for yourself?'

The footman lifted his head. 'I don't know what to say, my lord.'

'You can sit up straight, for starters!' barked Barnes.

Alfie sheepishly did so.

'First things first.' Lord Dalton began to pace back and forth. 'Alfie, I want you to know how proud I am of your swift actions.'

'My lord?' said Alfie, looking confused.

Tilly frowned.

'When Tilly fainted, your quick thinking in calling for help is just the type of response I would have hoped for. According to the doctor Tilly here has been working long hours and hasn't had enough sleep, causing exhaustion to get the better of her.'

Alfie raised an eyebrow.

Joyce tried to hide her smile.

'From now on, Tilly, I'd like you to take on some of the lighter duties, and get plenty of rest. I've already spoken to Barnes, and he's assured me it won't be a problem.'

'But I don't want to cause any disruption, my lord,' said Tilly.

Lord Dalton raised a hand. 'That's my final word on the matter. I hope you're not going to argue with me?'

'No, my lord,' said Tilly with a smile.

'As for you, Alfie. I've heard that one day you hope to become a butler?'

'Well, yes, my lord. One day. Eventually.' He looked at Barnes, who gave him a subtle wink.

'Barnes is going to start training you. It'll take some time. It's not a role you can learn overnight. It'll mean a very small pay rise. I hope that's to your satisfaction?'

Alfie could hardly contain his smile. 'Yes, my lord. Most definitely. Thank you.'

'Any questions?'

Alfie and Tilly looked at each other; both shook their heads. 'No, my lord.'

'In that case, that'll be all. Barnes, would you kindly show them out?'

'Yes, your lordship.' Barnes led the way. 'Come on, you two.'

After Barnes closed the door, Joyce looked fondly at Lord Dalton. 'What will you do when the baby arrives? Because arrive it surely will.'

Lord Dalton sighed. 'That's a bridge we'll cross when we come to it. I've asked Barnes to keep an eye on her. He'll inform me if there are any problems. Who knows? One day soon, Watermead Manor might welcome the pitter-patter of tiny feet. Isn't that a strange thought?'

'Thank you,' said Joyce.

Lord Dalton frowned. 'What for?'

'You know very well what for. Those two came in here convinced they were about to lose their positions.'

'I'm not a tyrant, you know. Well, maybe, a tiny bit of one,' he said with a smile.

'What is it?' asked Joyce with a chuckle. 'You're looking at me oddly.'

Lord Dalton frowned. 'My apologies, I've been somewhat blind.'

'How so?'

'You're a fine woman, Joyce. I only wish I'd seen it before. The doctor's a lucky man.'

Joyce blushed. 'It's still very early days with Dr Singer. We've really only just met, but it's going well.'

A noise made them both turn. Outside the study window the motorcar was returning along the drive.

'It looks like Fleming's back,' said Lord Dalton. 'I'd better see whether he has any news.'

'Indeed, you should,' said Joyce. 'And I'd better find something to distract me.'

CHAPTER FIFTEEN

L ord Dalton greeted Fleming's return on the manor house steps. Fleming had a grave look on his face. 'How was it in town, my friend?' he asked. 'Did you find the answers you were seeking?'

'I learned a lot, and not all of it's good. I'll need a moment to consider the facts, of which I've been told many over the last few days. There are those whose behaviour has surprised, alarmed, and disappointed me. All of this deceitfulness is the reason Gerald and Ackerman are now dead. I plan on ensuring they see justice.'

'If there's anything I can do to help, you need only ask.'

'I have to speak with Inspector Carp.'

'He was called away on another case.'

Fleming shook his head. 'The man should focus on the case at hand.' He entered the house, leaving Lord Dalton on the step. 'I'll take my rest now,' he mumbled to himself.

Lord Dalton sighed, feeling concerned by Fleming's displeasure. 'Thank you, Taylor. You can put the motorcar away now.'

'Very good, my lord.'

In the entrance hall, Lord Dalton found Fleming had not yet gone to his room. Instead, he watched Sir Peter talking to Ida. 'What's going on?' he asked. 'Is everything okay?'

'I think not. I feel I should intervene.'

Sir Peter put out his arm and placed it across the doorway, preventing Ida from leaving. 'Just hear me out. It's what Gerald would have wanted. If he were here, he wouldn't even have to consider it.'

'Get out of my way.' Ida attempted to push past.

'You're being unreasonable.'

'And you're being obnoxious. I won't be investing in this or any other expedition. Now, I insist you let me through!'

Sir Peter moved even closer.

'Excuse me,' said Fleming. 'What is this?'

'Yes. What the devil's going on?' Lord Dalton demanded.

'This man won't take no for an answer. He's been badgering me repeatedly to lend him money.'

'Invest,' corrected Sir Peter. 'Not lend. And I haven't been *badgering* anyone.'

'I would ask you to refrain from bothering Mrs Langley,' said Fleming. 'It's most ungentlemanly to intrude on her grief.'

Dr Singer arrived. 'Is everything all right? I heard the hubbub from the library. Are you okay, Ida?'

'I'm quite fine, thank you. I certainly don't need all these men running to my aid. I'm not some damsel in distress. I'm quite capable...' Ida began to sob.

Giving Sir Peter a steely glare, Dr Singer put an arm around her and escorted her away.

Sir Peter put up his hands. 'I'm sorry. Perhaps I overstepped?'

'There's no "perhaps" about it, Peter,' said Lord Dalton.

'I'll leave this with you, Anthony,' said Fleming. 'I must go to my room.'

MRS WINTERS and Joyce were sitting in the drawing room, eyeing one another. In an armchair behind them, Lady Stafford had been reading but was now fast asleep and gently snoring.

'You're bluffing,' said Mrs Winters.

'Perhaps,' said Joyce, holding her cards close.

'I can always tell when you're bluffing.'

'You always say that. Yet, I always win.'

'Nonsense. I win as often as you do.'

The two women laughed.

Joyce took a card and discarded one. She narrowed her eyes and put down her hand. 'Twenty-one!' she cried triumphantly.

'Are you sure you shuffled the pack properly?' joked Mrs Winters with a laugh. She looked up, and saw Dr Singer approaching. 'I think I'll take a stroll.' She collected the cards.

Joyce looked bemused, then spotted Dr Singer. 'How very subtle of you.'

'If he starts talking about sports cars, make sure you show an interest,' Mrs Winters advised with a smile. 'It might be dull to you, but men seem to love that sort of thing.'

Joyce giggled. 'I promise not to yawn too much.'

Dr Singer took the chair Mrs Winters had just vacated. 'I wondered whether you'd thought any more about Devon?'

'I'll have to check my diary when I return home, but I'm sure we can fix a time. I'd like that.'

Dr Singer smiled. 'As soon as I'm back, I'll get in touch and we can arrange the date.'

Fleming appeared behind them accompanied by Barnes and Lord Dalton. The three men conferred quietly, Fleming pointing at the sun terrace.

'What do you think that's all about?' said Dr Singer.

'I've no idea. It looks important, though. Mr Fleming looks very serious.'

MAJOR FIELDING SAT with Ida in the library, reading his newspaper while keeping one eye on the door for Sir Peter. He glanced over at her book of poetry. He'd tried poetry on and off over the years but had never understood the attraction. In his mind the poet rarely got to the point, just indulged in a lot of flowery shilly-shallying. Say what you mean and mean what you say had always been his motto.

'It's very kind of you, Major, but I'm sure you have better things to be doing with your time than babysitting me. I'm quite capable of looking after myself.'

'I know you are, my dear, but it would appear Sir Peter has no scruples. He seems to be circling like a starving vulture, and I won't stand for it. If I didn't have my standards, I'd box his ears.'

Ida chuckled.

'You have a very great sense of loyalty, don't you, Major?'

'I like to think so.' He folded his newspaper. 'What's happened to you shouldn't happen to anyone. I feel deeply saddened by it and if I can be of service to you, I hope you know I'm on hand anytime you need it. Have you any idea what you'll do next?'

'That's very generous of you. I haven't yet given much thought to the future. All my plans had been made together with Gerald, you see. Now it seems almost everyone wants a piece of his fortune, and there are so many expectations being placed upon me. I see now that it's something of a curse.'

Major Fielding stiffened. 'Might I make a suggestion?'

'Of course.'

'It occurs to me that you're feeling pressured to make decisions you're not ready to make, and to become someone you're not ready to be. However, you're young and, all being well, you have time on your side. You could simply do nothing. Continue as you were. You have financial security, thanks to Gerald, and I see a strong woman in front of me. Take your time.'

Ida smiled. 'Thank you, Major. I feel a little better. I'll consider what you suggest.'

Major Fielding puffed out his chest. 'My pleasure. I'm serious too. So, remember, should you require the services of a military man, who's more than a little past his prime, then you know who to contact.' He got to his feet. 'It's time for a pre-dinner cocktail. Would you care to join me?'

'That would be delightful.'

CHAPTER SIXTEEN

When guests arrived for pre-dinner drinks in the drawing room, they found a long banquet table had been arranged on the sun terrace outside the French doors. Barnes showed each of them to their allotted seat.

'This is all very exciting,' said Mrs Winters as she caught Barnes' attention. 'Champagne please, Barnes. Maybe a scotch and soda, too.'

Lady Stafford instructed Barnes to fetch her fur coat. 'I shall catch my death out here,' she insisted.

'Nonsense, it's a lovely evening,' said Mrs Winters.

'My hands and feet would argue otherwise.'

'I'm surprised they can get a word in, the way your mouth complains about everything,' said Mrs Winters under her breath, winking at Major Fielding.

Joyce sat beside the doctor. He immediately put

out a hand and squeezed hers. They smiled at each other and the doctor whispered something that made her blush.

'You two appear to be getting along exceedingly well,' observed Mrs Winters.

'You make a handsome couple, to be sure,' echoed Major Fielding. 'Fine indeed.'

Ida sat beside Lord Dalton, who scowled at Sir Peter as he arrived and sat away from them next to Dr Singer. He did his best to avoid eye contact with anyone, instead contenting himself with examining his gin glass.

When all the guests had arrived and were settled, Barnes brought a tray of drinks, including a jug of water, and then, to everyone's surprise, he returned to the house where he closed and locked the French doors behind him. It was apparent he did not plan on returning anytime soon.

The gathered guests looked at each other.

'How very odd,' said Major Fielding.

'Are we going to be playing a game?' asked Joyce. 'I love games.'

'This is outrageous! I demand to know what's going on. Is this your doing, Lord Dalton?' fumed Lady Stafford.

'Who's that?' asked Sir Peter.

Fleming had appeared from around a corner of the

terrace, dressed immaculately in a light grey woollen suit, shoes gleaming as he marched purposefully towards the guests. He checked the hour on his pocket watch, closed it, and slipped the precious timepiece back into his waistcoat.

'I believe it's Fleming,' said Dr Singer. 'He looks rather officious.'

At the sight of his friend, Lord Dalton chuckled to himself. 'This could get interesting,' he murmured to Ida.

'Why? What's happening?'

'You'll see.'

Fleming stood at the end of the table to address the guests. 'Ladies and gentlemen, thank you for your patience. I'm aware my summoning you here must seem quite peculiar. But, as will shortly become apparent, I have my reasons. Further, it's important that everyone remains seated for the duration. Also, if I give an instruction, it's imperative that it's followed and adhered to without question or hesitation.'

'Now things are really hotting up!' chuckled Mrs Winters.

'Duration of what?' asked Ida. 'I'm not entirely sure I have the stomach for many more surprises.'

Lord Dalton took her hand. 'It'll be fine. We'll get through this together.'

Fleming looked at each guest as he circled the long

table. 'I arrived at Watermead Manor to celebrate the union of Gerald and Ida Langley. It's fair to say, their sudden and secret marriage caused something of a stir. The young lovers had thrown caution to the wind and acted on what was in their hearts. Love. For me to see Gerald happy brought immense joy. His father and I shared an unshakable bond and upon his untimely death, I swore to protect his son.' His eyes met those of Lady Stafford. 'I'm heartbroken to say I failed both him, and Gerald. For reasons that seem inconceivable to me, there's someone among us who saw fit to take his life. And that of Vincent Ackerman, his accountant.'

Sir Peter sighed. 'Well, it wasn't me so, if you don't mind, I'm going to get myself another drink.' He held up his glass. 'This one seems to have vanished without trace.'

Fleming moved with lightning speed. Before Sir Peter could rise, he placed a firm hand on his shoulder. 'You will remain seated! You've shown yourself to be less than a gentleman on more than one occasion. Don't dishonour yourself any further.'

Sir Peter scowled, but did as he was bid.

Fleming resumed. 'I'll start with my good friend, Lord Anthony Dalton. After all, he is our most generous host this weekend.'

Lord Dalton looked confused, masking his nervousness with a smile.

'I hope that after this we can remain friends,' added Fleming.

Lord Dalton's smile instantly evaporated.

'You see, I realise now that I was invited under false pretences. Knowing how much Gerald values my opinion, Lord Dalton's hope was that I might discover something about Ida that would force me to act. He knows of my affection for the Langleys, and the promise I made to myself to safeguard Gerald's future. That would include informing Gerald of my concerns in the unlikely event that I thought his new wife was dishonest, or false in some way.'

Ida turned to Lord Dalton. 'Is this true? Did you really hope to jeopardise our marriage?'

Lord Dalton shook his head. 'It's not how it sounds, Ida. I'm not entirely sure what he's referring to.' He turned to Fleming. 'That's an outrageous accusation, Henry.'

'Unfortunately, a true one. You see, I had my suspicions when I heard the way you spoke of Ida. However, I knew for certain when, from a bedroom window, I saw you walking arm in arm with her across the lower garden; your affection was clear. It was immediately apparent to me your concerns were not for Gerald but for yourself. Your hints of Ida's not coming from money, or her habit of bettering herself by befriending those who could benefit her situation, and the question over Gerald's own ability to settle down, were mentioned to me not out of concern for him, but out of your own self-interest. Your hope was that I speak up and sow seeds of doubt in Gerald's mind.'

'What on earth would I have to gain by their unhappiness?'

'Everything!' Fleming looked his friend in the eye. 'You've fallen hopelessly in love with Ida.'

'What nonsense,' said Ida, looking to Lord Dalton to agree.

However, his face said it all. 'I'm sorry. I've been foolish and conducted myself shamefully.' Lord Dalton sank back in his seat. 'I fell in love with Ida without knowing it; my emotions have been in turmoil since Anne's death. You see, Ida wanted to join a humanitarian mission offering aid in Africa, and it was while arranging her trip that I developed deep feelings for her. Stupidly, I thought she'd come back with a realisation of all that we could be together. I never in a million years expected her to meet someone else. I should never have let her go. Once she met Gerald, I knew any chance I might have had was gone forever. My only hope was for her to turn to me, if Gerald could perhaps be convinced she wasn't right for him, or if he continued his bachelor lifestyle.' He hung his head. 'I feel utterly ashamed. I realise now, I'm still grieving, and have acted recklessly, irrationally and entirely inappropriately. I hope you'll all forgive me.'

JOYCE LOOKED at Fleming nervously as he rounded the table and approached her. 'You were aware of Lord Dalton's feelings towards Ida, weren't you?' he said.

'I could see Lord Dalton was lonely. Ida told me as much. These last few days I've also observed how she's toyed with his affections. As dear as she is to me, I don't like the way she behaves sometimes. Mrs Winters has expressed concerns for years but I'll admit I was blinkered to it, because Ida's my friend.'

Mrs Winters gave Joyce a look of loving concern.

Joyce continued. 'When I first heard Lord Dalton had invited both Gerald and Ida this weekend, I couldn't believe it. He must have been terribly upset to discover they'd married and I wasn't sure what he hoped to gain from throwing a celebration party. My initial thoughts had been that it showed him as a true gentleman. He put their happiness before his own. I still like to believe that to a certain degree that was the case.'

'Did you ever bring any of this up with Ida?'

'When I asked her how she felt about Lord Dalton, or his inviting her and Gerald this weekend, she didn't seem to understand my question. She certainly didn't consider how it might feel for him.'

'Did you argue?' asked Fleming.

'We never argued. *Ever.* Ida looked annoyed, then amused, when I mentioned it. She didn't want to talk about the past. It was as though anything that came before Gerald was irrelevant. Her focus was solely on him. As for this weekend, well, she wanted to have fun. Ida was happier than I'd ever seen her. She wanted to celebrate that.'

Ida wiped a tear from her eye. 'I'm sorry if I upset you. You know I'm a warm and caring person. Of course, I care about my past and everyone around me.'

'You can be all those things, and more, and I love you. I simply wonder whether I've ever seen the real you. I'm just not sure you're good for me any longer.'

'And you think I killed Gerald? Is that what you're saying, Joyce?'

Joyce looked pitifully at Lord Dalton. 'Maybe not you. But emotions shouldn't be trifled with. The ramifications of what someone else might do because of you, and your behaviour, are unknown.'

'DID Lord Dalton get rejected and then murder Gerald out of jealousy?' asked Sir Peter. 'Is that what this is all about?'

Fleming's face was sombre. 'That question kept me awake at night and troubled me greatly. The fact of the matter is that Lord Dalton made little attempt to hide his affection for Ida. Knowing the man as I do, I understood he wouldn't show his fondness for Ida so openly, had he committed such an act. Based on his recent behaviour, he can be accused of many things, but not murder.'

Sir Peter looked disappointed.

'Next we turn to Sir Peter Upton,' said Fleming. 'Who has attempted many times to part Gerald from his money for his numerous expeditions. Obviously, I'm aware you recently approached Ida with hopes of her funding an attempt to climb Mount Everest.'

'That was a misunderstanding. She's new to money. For the most part, rich types enjoy having their name associated with ground-breaking events.'

Fleming held an envelope aloft. 'In my hand, I have a letter from an acquaintance of mine. Colonel Charles Hubert.' He held up a second letter. 'Lady Clarisse Overton didn't hesitate to put her concerns in writing, either. She was exceedingly pleased you'd been tracked down. There are more letters on the way from many others who either financed your last expedition, or previous enterprises. I understand your last venture was to cross the Gobi desert using motorised transport?'

'That's right, it was quite a feat of endurance. Drought, hellish heat, extreme cold, dust, and wind, make it an immense challenge. I only just made it out alive.' He laughed and slapped the table as he appeared to picture the event.

Fleming wasn't smiling. 'Only, there's no evidence of you taking part in any expedition. In fact, I have it on good authority, you were in New York at the time you claim to have been crossing the Gobi.'

Sir Peter shifted uneasily. 'There must be some mistake.'

'There's no mistake, Sir Peter. *You* are a charlatan. A con man. You've financed a lavish lifestyle based on lies. Colonel Hubert and Lady Overton are very keen to speak to you. In fact, the colonel is sending two of his men to pick you up.'

Sir Peter leapt to his feet. 'In that case, I'll bid you all farewell.' He ran across the terrace to the side of the house, where he stumbled straight into the arms of two men in uniform coming the other way. The soldiers strong-armed Sir Peter into a waiting car and he could still be heard loudly protesting as he was driven away.

'He'll be questioned by the colonel who supported his venture, not only with his own personal money, but with equipment supplied by the military. Once the army's satisfied, he'll be passed to civilian police for further questioning.'

'Goodness me!' said Major Fielding. 'He'd been cajoling me for a few shillings, too. I told the man he's barking up the wrong tree. I have little more than my service pension.'

Fleming turned to Major Fielding. 'It would seem neither Lord Dalton, nor Sir Peter, are alone in having secrets.'

CHAPTER SEVENTEEN

Major Fielding took out his pipe and began stuffing it with tobacco. 'Secrets you say?' He raised his colossal eyebrows and stared at Fleming. 'I suppose we all have them in one shape or form.'

'I checked with Lord Dalton and he assures me that it was you who insisted on visiting the manor this weekend. Yet, during your interview, you suggested it was the other way around, and that he invited you. If, as you claim, you've never met either Ida or Gerald before, why would you insist on being present at their marriage celebration this weekend?'

The major, having successfully lit his pipe, released a thick cloud of fragrant tobacco smoke. Using his pipe to point at Fleming, he said, 'Are you sure that's what I said?'

'I'm quite certain.'

He pondered a moment, smoking and observing Fleming as though considering what the enemy's tactics might be before a military campaign. 'There's no real mystery. It's true I'm aware of Gerald and his parents, Mary and Jonathan Langley. We all read about their demise on the ship returning from Ireland.'

'But there's more, isn't there?'

'Not really,' said the major unconvincingly.

'Is it not true, your wife and son, Fiona and Edward, were on the same ship that sank in the Irish sea the night Mr and Mrs Langley lost their lives? Were they not also travelling back from Ireland that night?'

The major's eyes glazed with tears. He took out the tattered photograph of his wife and son. 'My wife was of Irish descent. She was visiting family. My young son, Edward, was with her. The small privately owned ship was meant to have departed earlier than it did but, at the captain's discretion, it waited almost an hour for Mr and Mrs Langley to arrive. The captain knew his wealthy passengers well and so he waited.'

'This delay proved catastrophic,' said Fleming.

Major Fielding nodded. 'According to one of the few surviving crew members, concerns had been raised that any delay could put the ship in the path of a storm that had been forecast and which, in the event, turned out to be of a magnitude far greater than reported. The wait meant the doomed ship sailed directly into it, and only three out of nearly a hundred and ninety-two passengers and crew survived. Fiona and Edward weren't among them.'

'I'm sorry for your loss, Major. Though nobody can be certain, it's possible that had it not been for the delay, many lives wouldn't have been lost that night, including your wife's and son's. I must ask why you would lie about your connection to the Langleys?'

The major didn't hesitate. He reached into his jacket and pulled out a small pistol, which he laid on the table.

Joyce gasped at the sight.

The doctor jumped to his feet.

'Please be calm,' said Fleming. 'The major has no ill-intent towards anyone here.'

The major muttered his agreement. 'For a long time, I resented Gerald. Because of his parents and the actions of the ship's captain, I lost my wife and boy. Through determination, and pure bloody-mindedness, I pushed the heartache to the back of my mind. Then, when I learned he'd married something within me snapped. As some bizarre act of revenge, I planned on shooting him dead, and to hell with the consequences. When it came to it, and I met the chap, I couldn't go through with it. He was too likeable. I imagined him to be the sort my boy, Edward, who would now be a grown man, would have enjoyed the company of.'

'All the same, Digby, a loaded gun isn't the sort of thing to have at the dinner table,' admonished Lord Dalton.

Fleming held out his open hand. In the palm were the bullets from the major's pistol. 'You needn't fear. During our first dinner together, I noticed from the shape of the major's suit that he was concealing a weapon. During my search of his room I discovered the gun under his mattress and removed the bullets. I had wondered why he should carry a pistol, but when I saw him share the photograph of his family with Mrs Winters I sensed a deep sadness behind the story he presented. I made some enquiries, and soon learned the details of their tragic passing. I was able to confirm that on the same ship's manifest as Mr and Mrs Langley were two passengers with the same surname as Major Fielding. I realised my instincts had been correct; the major possibly carried a grudge.'

The major stiffened his lip. He kissed the photograph and put it away in his pocket. 'I'm a military man to my bones, trained to kill in the white-hot heat of battle, but to look a man in the eye and *murder* in cold blood? I just couldn't do it; couldn't dishonour the memory of my wife and boy in that way. God rest their souls.'

Henry Fleming strode around the table, the seated guests following his every move with their eyes. He stopped at Lady Stafford. 'From the very beginning, you made your opinion clear: Ida wasn't good enough for Gerald. Having known you as long as I have, it didn't surprise me one jot. You've always had exceedingly high standards. Standards you expected Gerald to uphold.

'However, for your own sake, what concerned me was the possibility that your dislike for Ida might end with your ejection from what had become your home, the Langleys' estate, Chippingwood Hall. If you were to force his hand, Gerald would most certainly choose Ida over you and, for the sake of their happiness, insist you leave their residence.

'Having foreseen this possibility yourself, it was important you gained some advantage. It was this that led you to secretly examine Gerald's financial accounts. It was then that you stumbled upon Vincent Ackerman's dishonesty.'

'He'd been stealing,' said Lady Stafford. She held her head up high. 'I uncovered his deceit.'

'Yet, you didn't go directly to Gerald with this information,' stated Fleming.

'Why should I? Gerald was being foolish.'

'Instead, you planned to blackmail Vincent Ackerman into ensuring adequate funds were made available to you in the event you were forced out of Chippingwood Hall.'

'I deserved it. I'd given up my life and own home to look after Gerald. There was a very real possibility he could have left me destitute.'

'When Gerald suddenly died, both you and Ackerman became desperate to cover up the misappropriated money.'

'It would seem that with both Gerald and Mr Ackerman gone, my future is in the hands of the woman I sought to banish from my godson's life.' She refused to look in Ida's direction. 'Certainly, the kind of sting in the tail I hadn't anticipated.'

Margaret Winters sipped the last drops of her champagne and, in the absence of a butler, footman, or other serving staff, poured herself another. 'I suppose I'm to be accused of some horrendous lie, or insidious act as well, am I, Mr Fleming?'

'Your transgression was a deed perpetrated out a sense of loyalty to Joyce. You were concerned Joyce might have poisoned Gerald out of jealousy.'

'Joyce didn't know Gerald. Why would I think she murdered him?'

'Yet, she did know him, didn't she? Gerald had met

Joyce at the annual Southern Summer Ball where you'd hoped some romance might have blossomed between them. However, it was the confident and beautiful Ida, who Joyce had invited to accompany her, who took the initiative and danced most of the evening with Gerald.'

'What of it?'

'The summer ball was the catalyst. It meant that when the meeting between Ida and Gerald occurred in Kenya he was already smitten. A trip, I might add, encouraged by Joyce, little knowing Ida's true motive, and paid for by Lord Dalton.'

'I'm sure the prior meeting at the summer ball had some bearing on it, but I really couldn't say for certain. What exactly are you getting at?'

'I had wondered how a decorative cocktail glass found its way into Lord Dalton's room. I realised it couldn't have been there long because a maid, while attending to the room, would have noticed and picked it up. The only explanation was that it had been put there the morning of the interviews. It became clear to me that having collected the cocktail glass at the time of the murder, while everyone's attention was on Gerald, you slipped the glass carefully into your bag.'

'Why would I do that?'

'You realised there was a chance, no matter how remote, that Joyce had laced Gerald's drink with poison.'

'Joyce would never do such a thing. Why would I think that she'd harm Gerald? I certainly don't meddle in her personal life.'

'Come now. We've seen how protective you are of Joyce. You adore the girl. I can quite imagine how she would have laid bare her feelings to you, her life governess who she considers her friend and confidante. Her outpouring of unfairness, the injustice, at being passed over time and again, when all the while Ida so easily garnered the affections and interest of so many eligible men.

'You panicked. Frantic and unsure how to dispose of the glass, which remained in your handbag, you decided it must be placed in another room, anywhere away from your own. You took the glass from your handbag, and crossed the hall to hide it in Lord Dalton's bedroom. His was the nearest unlocked door.'

'I've never been in Lord Dalton's room. I'm not quite sure what you're suggesting.'

'Yet, I'm certain you have. When I examined Lord Dalton's room, my nose caught the scent of a very distinctive perfume, which I also smelled in the hallway. It was when I entered your room that I knew for certain it was you who planted the glass to draw my attention away from you, and Joyce. I'm not suggesting your intention had been to point the finger at Lord

Dalton. You were merely acting as the protective governess.

'I repeat, you had no intention of framing Lord Dalton, it was just that his happened to be the nearest unlocked door when you needed to dispose of the glass with haste.'

Mrs Winters looked at Joyce. 'I know in my heart you'd never harm anyone, but I panicked when I saw Gerald collapse and drop his glass. I'm not sure what I was thinking but, in that moment, I feared you may have attempted to poison Ida, and Gerald was poisoned by mistake! When I found myself with Gerald's glass, I was terrified that, should I be discovered with it, I might find myself accused. So I hid it.'

Dr Singer put out a comforting hand to Joyce. 'In the short time I've known you, I can see what a caring soul you are. I saw first-hand your empathy towards Tilly. A person so full of kindness couldn't have harmed Gerald. In fact, I'm not sure anyone here is capable of such a thing. It was most likely an accident, wouldn't you say, Fleming? Or maybe, despite what Inspector Carp says, it was one of those jazz musicians. Gerald may have crossed one of them without even knowing it, while on a trip to London, for example. I've heard many such stories of revenge.'

Fleming regarded him sternly and the doctor fell silent.

Henry took out his pocket watch and opened the case. He stood silently, seemingly lost in thought, examining the precious timepiece.

'Mr Fleming?' prompted Joyce.

He bent down beside her and spoke quietly. 'Thank you, Joyce. I was remembering somebody close to me. Somebody who gave me strength in the darkest of times. This investigation pains me greatly, and I wanted to remind myself of her strength.' He discreetly turned the pocket watch towards Joyce to reveal what was inside the case.

Joyce immediately understood and placed a gentle hand on his.

The guests waited.

Fleming rose and circled the table once more.

Almost a minute passed, then Fleming raised his eyes. He snapped shut the case of the pocket watch and carefully tucked it back into his waistcoat.

'It's interesting to me that you, Dr Singer, should want to cast suspicion elsewhere. It's as if you sense you no longer have anywhere to hide.'

All heads turned towards the doctor.

Dr Singer forced a laugh. 'Is that a joke? Are you suggesting I had something to do with Gerald's death?'

'I'm not suggesting anything,' Fleming said. 'I'm stating it with certainty.'

CHAPTER EIGHTEEN

Dr Robert Singer turned to Joyce, and the others at the table. 'Don't believe a word of it. It's inconceivable I should do such a thing. For a start, what do I possibly have to gain from his death?'

'We'll come to that, Doctor,' said Fleming.

'Are you quite sure about this, Henry?' asked Lord Dalton. 'We're talking about a doctor having committed murder? A man who's taken the Hippocratic oath!'

'Though the second murder is a little more complicated, he is in fact guilty of two murders. We must not forget that poor Vincent Ackerman also met a terrible and untimely end.'

'I don't believe it,' said Ida. 'I've known Robert for years. He simply wouldn't do such a thing.'

'Let's examine the facts,' said Fleming. 'On the

evening of Gerald's death, we were all enjoying wonderful music from a jazz band. Gerald and Ida were on the terrace dancing, as were Dr Singer and Joyce. It appeared the doctor and Joyce had quickly formed an attachment and I'll admit that, although my attention was for the most part on the newlyweds, I did fleetingly wonder whether this new friendship might blossom into something more.

'When the jazz band had to leave, our attention turned to Lord Dalton, who wished to make a speech, but Dr Singer suggested Gerald should say a few words first. It was also around this time that Ida knocked a bottle of champagne off the sideboard. While our attention was elsewhere, the doctor hastily placed two drinks on a tray, one of which he discreetly laced with the deadly strychnine poison. He made a very public show of collecting two more random drinks from the table, then offered the tray in such a way that Joyce and Ida took the drinks closest to them, leaving the remaining two drinks for Gerald and himself. The plan being that Gerald would take the glass closest to him. However, as luck would have it, the slightly drunk and joyous Gerald, not only took his own cocktail and drank it down, but also Dr Singer's. To further embellish his deceit, the doctor jokingly feigned protest. Moments later, as we know, Gerald was dead.'

Ida let out a sob.

'It was then, however, that a problem occurred, requiring the doctor to think on his feet.

'His plan was that while panic ensued, the glass which had delivered the poisoned cocktail was to be removed, leaving no evidence of wrong-doing and no chance of the glass being traced back to him. However, Mrs Winters put paid to that. Fearing Joyce may have had a hand in the poisoning and, having seen Gerald drop the glass, she picked it up and put it in her handbag then, as we now know, later took the opportunity to hide it in Lord Dalton's room.

'So, unable to find the glass and remove the evidence as he'd hoped, the doctor panicked; and this is when he faked his own poisoning. As you'll recall, he began to shake and choke, then collapsed exactly as Gerald had done. It was during this display that he fell and smashed many glasses, no doubt hoping one of them held the evidence of poison. The glass I later found beneath the table had simply rolled there during this performance and was of no consequence.'

Fleming adjusted his cufflinks and straightened his jacket before continuing. 'During his interview, the doctor mentioned his hope that he and Gerald would become friends. This was a lie. Knowing what he had to do, he couldn't allow himself to befriend Gerald. His unexpected, and irrepressible, attraction for Joyce, I believe, is the only time these past few days the doctor has let his guard down and allowed himself to be genuine.

'And there were, of course, the minute and telltale signs of crushed strychnine pills I discovered within the carved edge of the rosewood dresser in your room. Despite your best efforts to hide the truth from me, the evidence will always find you out.'

Dr Singer slowly applauded. 'In this fantasy of yours, what of poor Vincent Ackerman? Why would I have wanted him dead? I barely even knew the man.'

'It was something Ackerman told me that sparked my interest. Shortly after his arrival at Watermead Manor, he was working in the study adjacent to the library and, whilst poring over his accounting, he overheard two voices. Voices he didn't recognise, of that I'm certain. At the time this meant little to him but, after Gerald's death, it suddenly had great significance. Convinced he'd heard the plotting of the murder, he felt he needed to bring it to someone's attention. What was said, remains a mystery, but it was enough to unwittingly cause his own death.'

'You make it all sound feasible, I suppose. However, the powder in my room could have been planted by anyone to implicate me. Just as anyone could have laced Gerald's drink. I would argue that I was genuinely ill and collapsed, unfortunately smashing glasses in the process. And, just for the record, I do have feelings for Joyce, she's a terrific girl.'

'Lies, lies, lies, lies, Dr Singer!' raged Fleming. 'You lie so often you can no longer differentiate fact from fiction. Yet, I see your evil actions as plain as day.'

'In that case, how on earth could I have been in two places at once? That's the one huge flaw in your otherwise tremendous theory. I was with *Ida* at the time of Vincent Ackerman's murder. Explain that away, *if* you can.'

Fleming's eyes narrowed. 'With pleasure, Doctor. You didn't work alone, did you?' He turned and pointed a finger. 'Ida was your accomplice!'

A gasp came from those around the table.

Fleming's anger was close to spilling over, but he kept his composure and pressed on. 'It was she who murdered Vincent Ackerman.'

'But, Henry, Ida was in her bed when it happened,' said Lord Dalton.

'Yes, *pretending* to be overcome with grief,' insisted Fleming, 'while Dr Singer *claimed* to be sitting with her. Thus, he gave them both an alibi, even refusing Joyce the chance to check on Ida when she requested a visit.'

'That's true,' agreed Joyce.

'Yet, Ida wasn't in her room. She was committing the second, but necessary, murder of Ackerman. The very man who unwittingly brought his concerns to her and so sealed his fate.'

Dr Singer no longer smiled confidently. His eyes were fixed on Ida's and hers on his.

'I don't understand, Henry,' said Lord Dalton. 'If this is true, what's their motive?'

'Money. They committed these unspeakable crimes for financial gain. Ida's ambition has always been to shake off her underprivileged upbringing and live the wealthy lifestyle she so coveted. She saw the likes of you, Anthony, Gerald, and even Joyce, enjoying life with very little concern for money. Doctor Singer, I'm sorry to say, was an unwilling partner in these crimes. He had no choice but to participate.

'When Ida first met Gerald at the Southern Summer Ball, she realised he was instantly attracted to her. Seeing her opportunity for the wealth and position she'd always wanted, she hatched her plan. Knowing a secret about the doctor, she blackmailed him into assisting her. No doubt also promising him money, as well as her silence, in exchange. Equally, if he did not help her, she threatened to reveal his wrong-doing and destroy his life.'

Sweating profusely now, the doctor loosened his tie.

'You told me of your brother's troubles,' said Fleming. 'How, due to an underlying illness, he lost his job.

What you neglected to tell me was how you falsified his medical records, claiming he was fit to work. He needed a clean bill of health to ensure he remained employed as a freight train mechanic. His condition was far worse than you reported, wasn't it?'

'I misrepresented his condition in medical reports,' admitted Doctor Singer. 'In fact, one night he blacked out while moving carriages and someone was killed.'

'While it's true your intentions had been good, the falsified medical reports left you open to blackmail when Ida discovered what you'd done and threatened to report you. Your medical licence would be revoked, and imprisonment was a real possibility.'

The doctor nodded. 'I confided in her because I thought she was my friend, but she used it against me. Manipulated me the way she does everyone. Of course, I shouldn't have done what I did but my brother needed that job. He literally begged me for help; he had a young family to support! I defy anyone to have acted differently. My mistake was not in helping my brother but in trusting *her*.'

Ida remained defiant. 'You've no idea how it pains me to see those born into wealth flaunting their money and revelling in the freedom it offers. Merely by being born to the right parents they're able to live a carefree life, while the rest of us struggle to make ends meet. Gerald's fortune was handed to him on a silver platter, without him having to lift a finger. He was entitled and thoroughly spoiled. Why shouldn't I take it? He was no more deserving than either myself, Sir Peter, Major Fielding, or yourself, for that matter. I'd initially thought I could divorce him after a few years and take a large portion of the money that way, but I discovered from Ackerman that wasn't possible; a document he had me sign saw to that. I was left with no choice. If I was to be finally happy, I had to kill him. I just couldn't do it alone without raising suspicion.'

Fleming gritted his teeth. 'It was no coincidence you met Gerald in Kenya, was it? You actually orchestrated it! A woman like you can't risk leaving her future in the hands of fate; that's far too dangerous. And so, once Gerald was hooked, you heartlessly used Dr Singer to remove him from the equation and put you in control of his vast wealth and your own destiny.'

'What was I thinking?' asked Doctor Singer. 'What have we done?'

'We did what we had to,' snapped Ida. 'You simply needed some coercion.'

The doctor poured himself a glass of water. His hand shaking, he gulped it down and poured another, staring straight at Joyce. 'I was falling in love with you, Joyce. Truly I was.' Taking a small tin from his jacket pocket, he deftly poured a powder into the glass, which he stirred with his finger. 'We would have been good together, Joyce. I'm so very sorry.'

'Don't do it,' screamed Joyce.

Realising what was about to happen, Fleming sprang towards Dr Singer, but it was too late. The doctor drank down the powdered strychnine, lurched to his feet and walked unsteadily across the lawn in the direction of the lake.

The major was about to stop him when Fleming placed a hand on his shoulder. 'Let him go. It's over for him now.'

Dr Singer didn't make it far. He stood for a moment on the lush green lawn, looking up at the sky. Moments later, he collapsed to his knees, fell heavily forward and didn't move again.

Fleming raised a hand and Barnes unlocked the French doors. An earlier phone call to Scotland Yard, requesting a message be sent to Inspector Carp, had reached him in the nick of time. He now appeared, flanked by a police constable carrying handcuffs.

'I'd do it all again, you know. The gamble was worth it.'

'You're a fine actress, Ida, and you put on a brave face, but I don't believe you,' said Fleming.

She looked towards Dr Singer's body. 'I did black-mail him. Robert was never going to amount to much on his own. He needed cornering and prodding into action.' Ida stood arrogantly, looking at each guest in turn. 'This is it, then. It seems the only thing in my plan I hadn't accounted for was the great mind of Henry Fleming. Bravo, sir!'

Fleming showed no emotion, only watched impassively as Ida was led away by the constable.

'Perhaps the ladies could be helped inside,' said Fleming, stoically.

'Of course,' said Lord Dalton, beckoning Barnes to assist. 'Perhaps, if everyone could follow me. Barnes will arrange some refreshment to steady our nerves.'

Wearily, everyone got to their feet and went into the house. Fleming remained outside on his own for a while longer.

Inspector Carp joined him. 'You did it again, Fleming.'

'Indeed I did,' he said.

'Why the long face, my friend? You should be celebrating.'

'There's little to celebrate, Inspector. My findings won't bring Gerald back, nor Vincent Ackerman. This whole case is a calamity. Even my good friend, Lord Dalton, didn't come out of it unblemished.'

'Unfortunately, it's the nature of what we do. There's usually always some unavoidable collateral damage,' said Carp.

'While digging for the truth, we unearth many lies.'

'You can't be judged for that.'

'Yet, I judge myself, Inspector. I must always hold myself to the highest standards.' He looked Inspector Carp in the eye. 'I have no choice but to put the truth above all else. If I don't, where will we be?'

The two men stood in silence for a moment before Fleming asked, 'What of the case you were called away to investigate?'

'Does that brain of yours never rest? It was straight forward enough, even for me! I won't bore you with the details.'

'Inspector Carp, you should know me well enough by now to know the details could never bore me, for they are of the essence. One of these days, I shall ask you to acquaint me with the case and insist you start at the very beginning, leaving out not a single one of those details.'

CHAPTER NINETEEN

The church bells rang, confetti filled the air and, as the bride and groom appeared through the church doors, the waiting guests whooped and cheered. The happy couple worked their way past friends and family, who shook their hands and kissed them as they went.

Joyce hugged Tilly. 'Congratulations. You look beautiful,' she whispered.

Tilly gave a little pirouette, the lace trimmed tulle skirt of her wedding dress swirling around her ankles. 'Do you think so?'

'You're radiant.' She turned to Alfie. 'You look after your new wife, and the baby. You hear?'

'I will, I promise. Thank you for everything.'

'Don't thank me. All this is down to Lord Dalton.

I think he's as excited as anyone about this wedding and soon to be welcoming a baby at Watermead.'

'You're right,' Tilly giggled. 'He's suggested hiring a nursemaid to help with all the duties.' She looked over Joyce's shoulder. 'Here he comes now.'

'Look at you, Tilly,' said Lord Dalton. 'Pretty as a picture.' He shook Alfie's hand. 'Well done, lad.'

Tilly and Alfie moved on through the guests until they eventually climbed into the back of a waiting car.

After a toot of the horn by the chauffeur, they were driven away.

'I gave them the weekend off. Hopefully, we'll cope,' said Lord Dalton with a smile.

Joyce took his arm. 'You're far too generous,' she said teasingly.

'You know, I'm not good at these types of decisions. Perhaps I should have allowed them longer? The lady of the house would usually be able to advise.'

'No,' said Joyce.

'What?' said Lord Dalton.

'It's too soon,' she laughed. 'You agreed to give me a full year.'

'You must allow me some hope that you'll soon become Lady Dalton.'

Joyce smiled mischievously. She stood up on tiptoes and gave him a peck on the cheek. 'Surely it's a lady's prerogative to keep her man guessing.'

'So, I'm your man, at least? That sounds promising.'

Joyce laughed and squeezed his arm.

HENRY FLEMING SAT in his armchair at Avonbrook Cottage reading a telegram. He mumbled something incoherent and Skip, who lay dozing at his feet, wagged his tail and looked up at the sound of Fleming's murmurs.

'Is everything okay?' asked Fleming's housekeeper.

'It would seem, Mrs Clayton, that the short break I'd hoped for is to be interrupted.'

Mrs Clayton smiled to herself. 'Another case, is it?'

'Unfortunately, yes.' He glanced fleetingly at her. 'Are you smiling? This is no laughing matter. I was looking forward to some time off.' His attention returned to the telegram.

'I know you were. But, if you don't mind my saying, you can get a little peevish if your mind isn't occupied.' She set down a cup of strong tea on a small side-table. 'There you go. I put two sugars in it for you; you need to keep your strength up. Now, drink it while it's hot.'

He looked up. 'I'm sorry, did you say something? Who's peevish?'

Mrs Clayton pretended not to hear. 'I've made a cherry cake. Would you like a slice?' She waited just outside the door and counted in her head. '1... 2... 3... 4...'

'Mrs Clayton, I need to send an urgent telegram. When I return, I'd better pack a small case.'

'I'll fetch the case,' she sighed. She could hear movement in the front room and Fleming gently asking Skip to move out of the way. 'C'mon, boy, I've work to do.'

Thank you for choosing this Henry Fleming mystery. I hope you enjoyed it and will return for Death on Damson Island.

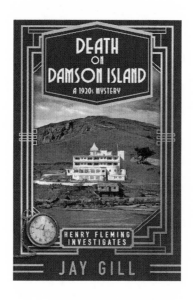

Henry Fleming Investigates
Murder in Fulbridge Village
The Mystery of Watermead Manor
Death on Damson Island

Inspector James Hardy
Chilling British Crime Thrillers
Caution: This series contains occasional strong

language, moderate violence, and mild sexual
references.

Knife & Death

Angels

Hard Truth

Inferno

Killing Shadows

Don't Go Home

Inspector Hardy Box Set, Books 1-3

Inspector Hardy Box Set, Books 4-6

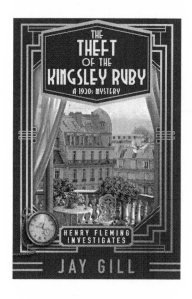

Never miss out, sign up to my mailing list on my website, and join me on Facebook, Instagram and more.

Jay Gill Newsletter
www.jaygill.net
Facebook Author Page
facebook.com/jaygillauthor
Instagram
instagram.com/jaygillauthor
Twitter
twitter.com/jaygillauthor

Made in the USA
Middletown, DE
06 September 2022

73267614R00120